Never Get Old

By
Erock

ISBN: 978-0-9906647-2-7

Author Contact Information
Email: misfitmountianmedia@yahoo.com

"Down in My Heart" by George Willis Cooke – Public Domain

Cover Photo: "Frida"
Dr. David Palmini
www.sanohospital.com

Author Photo Credit
Jonny Edward
www.jonnyedward.com

To Alvin

The Where

CHAPTER I

Welcome to Midland City. Midland City is in the middle of everything. Literally. Midland City is geographically, socially, economically, culturally, racially and politically in the middle. Completely centric. It is the home to more three star hotels and three star restaurants per capita than any other city in the world. Middle of the road is exactly why tourists flock here. They know that they will not be wowed, but nor will they be disappointed. No risk. Everything is 50/50 in Midland City. Unless, that is, you are unfortunate enough to wind up at the Midland City Dog Shelter. Then you have a 98 percent chance of death. The Midland City Chamber of Commerce does not put that tidbit of information anywhere in their visitor's guide.

"Alvin! Alvin! Alvin, wake up!" shouts Bruce, the Manager of the City Dog Shelter.

Bruce is a stout, dark bearded, pear-shaped man with beady eyes and abnormally large ears. Bruce's destiny came-to-pass because of low math scores on his S.A.T. test in high school. He had the choice of either going to Midland Community College where he could study to be a paralegal, or get an entry-level position at the Midland City Dog Shelter. He chose the shelter, much to his mother's dismay. He did it because, at the time, the benefits of the shelter job were two-fold. First, he'd have free time before and after work so it wouldn't interfere with his obsessive/compulsive habit of collecting little bars of soap from hotels around the world.

Bruce doesn't remember why he started collecting miniature hotel soaps. It began when he was quite young. Bruce has never been to any of the hotels that the soaps are from. He acquires them by either writing a heartfelt letter to the manager of the hotel, or he just simply purchases them online. The collecting aspect of his hobby is pretty simple, really.

The second benefit of going immediately into the workforce was that he would finally be able to move out of his parent's attic. He liked living in their attic because it was free, but he hated living in it because the roof leaked. Even though he stored his little soaps carefully wrapped in tissue paper and then double-boxed in plastic tubs, the constant fear of them getting damaged by water was debilitating for him. Like all free men, Bruce knows that living in fear isn't really living.

So Bruce took the job and never looked back. Ten years later, his miniature bar soap collection numbers well over 8,000.

Because of the high employee burn out rate and subsequent high employee turnover at the shelter, Bruce has climbed the "dog shelter ladder of success" very quickly. Nevertheless, he wasn't ever quite able to make the leap out of his parents' attic. Nor did he make the leap of being able to learn how to do his own laundry or cook his own meals or even how to clean himself properly. His mother cries and cries and cries. His selfish laziness will drive her to an early grave. The moment that happens, Bruce is moving downstairs to where the "good" television is. The one with a remote control that actually works.

Bruce is wearing dirty, city issued blue overalls that say "Midland City Dog Shelter" in bold, white lettering. Underneath that, it says "Bruce" in red lettering. Underneath "Bruce" it says "Manager of Midland City Dog Shelter," in a sharp bold white; just in case you somehow didn't read "Midland City" in the top part. Yes, it is redundant in its redundancy. But so is Bruce's job.

"Alvin! Wake up! Alvin?"

Bruce is calling out to Alvin, who lays sleeping alone in a cage. It is a cage among hundreds of cages exactly like his. Dirty, cold, and a little rusty. A cage devoid of blankets and toys. A cage containing a metal bowl half-filled with warm water and another metal bowl offering the remnants of sub-par dog food. Sub-par dog food made especially for unfortunate dogs like Alvin. Food made from road-kill de jour and the remains of other, unfortunate dogs. Alvin does not stir, but sleeps on, dreaming of nothing in particular. Alvin is comfortable with who he is. His genuine authenticity affords him the peace of mind to block out both Bruce and the deafening din created by the relentless barking of two hundred frightened dogs. Alvin is also mostly deaf and slips into a near coma every time he falls asleep, so that is working to his advantage right now.

Alvin is a seven-pound silver-dapple miniature dachshund who, obviously, has had a rough stretch at some point during his life. His semi-mangy black coat is speckled with brown and silver spots and a mask of aged-white has conquered his face and ears long ago. Flakey dried crusts of bodily fluids encircle Alvin's cloudy, bloodshot eyes, and his dry tongue hangs out of his toothless mouth. He is neither neglected nor abused. On the contrary. His life and living conditions, up until a few days ago, were very nice.

"Wake up, Alvin," coaxes Bruce, poking at him rather rudely with his right index finger. "It's time to go."

Alvin has a brief asthma attack, as is his morning routine, and opens his eyes to face a new day. Technically, although he goes through the motions of opening his eyes, he is mostly blind, so it is more or less pointless as far as the practicality of it all. He can see a little bit. Close up. Sort of. If he squints. Sometimes. But mostly not so much. He has cataracts on top of glaucoma on top of the fact that he is just really really really old and body parts just sort of get worn out and don't work so great anymore. It's a fact of life. For everyone.

Right now at least, it is good that Alvin can't see or hear the breadth and scope of the dog pound. It would depress him. Which is pretty difficult to do. Alvin maintains a very positive attitude at all times. That's just who he is.

With great initial effort, due to his crippling arthritis, Alvin slowly rises. His legs are wobbly and make popping sounds emanate from his joints. It's painful to watch. Once completely upright and balanced, Alvin wags his tail with the energy of an eight-week old puppy. Even with all of his health issues and his current state of affairs, Alvin is the happiest living being in the universe. He is full of love and life and kindness and joy. Alvin's only burning desire is to love everyone and everything he comes in contact with, and he does it unconditionally and wholly. He was born to please and does it naturally. He is, truly and literally, man's best friend.

"Your three days are up," explains Bruce, as if Alvin would understand and maybe have something to say about it. "Sorry, boy."

Bruce's words mean nothing to Alvin. As far as Alvin knows, he is going to be given breakfast. Alvin would like breakfast. He is eager to receive some sub-par dog food.

When Alvin was younger, at the puppy mill, his breakfast would consist of dog poop and shredded newspaper, but for the past ten years his breakfast consisted of a warm, homemade mush that tasted like lamb or beef or chicken or sometimes fish. The mush was particularly convenient since all of Alvin's teeth were rotten and had to be surgically removed. Before he was rescued, the rotten teeth had given him a nasty infection that almost killed him. Almost. But not quite. He was rescued and got medical treatment just in time. He was one of the lucky ones, for sure. Then he got even luckier when he was adopted and afforded the luxury of a home, attention, a bed and love. And, boy oh boy, Alvin especially loved his new mush food.

Now that he has been taken from his owner and put in this cage, the food is still pleasantly mushy, but tastes like something odd. Not lamb or beef or chicken or fish, but some other kind of meat. Sort of. A mystery meat.

"But,"thought Alvin, moments after he tasted it for the first time and felt discouraged, "at least it is meat. At least it is not shredded newspaper and poop."

So Alvin doesn't mind. Even if he did mind, Alvin doesn't get discouraged for very long. Alvin is a survivor. Alvin emerged from the depths of Hell to live in the glory of the best of what life has to offer. Or, at least that's how it was looking up until this point.

One thing that troubles Alvin is that he doesn't know where his owner is. He has not seen her in three days. He is worried about her. He hopes that she is okay. He was taken from their home and brought here by a strange and very good-smelling man with incredibly soft hands. He does not know why. He doesn't mind it here too badly, but it is starting to remind him of his old life at the puppy mill. All the barking dogs and very little human contact unnerve him a bit. In addition, he can smell the fear in all of the other dogs. The smell of fear is an ugly smell. Alvin knows that the smell fear is a worrisome smell at best.

Nevertheless, the mornings here are still much nicer than the mornings at the puppy mill. Here, he gets food and water. Here, he knows that he is going to wake up in the morning. He will never forget the time he woke up at the puppy mill, and five of the dogs sharing his tiny, rusted, filthy cage (an old chicken coop, actually) had frozen to death overnight. Their bodies were frozen solid, their eyes wide open with horror and incrusted with ice crystals. Almost one third of his cage mates died while he slept, and their bodies were not removed for a week. Rats began to eat them. Rats ate their frozen eyes. Alvin will never forget the terror of that week. Unfortunately, he could still see really well back then.

Worst of all, Alvin couldn't do anything about it. He couldn't even turn away. His jaw was wired to the cage so that he wouldn't fight with the other dogs that were crammed in there. So he just had to watch. Watch the rats devour his dead cage mates. Wondering if he would be next.

That was years and years ago and now it is breakfast time. He's not at home, but he's somewhere that has food, so Alvin is excited. Happy. Full of anticipation. So full, in fact, that he lowers his shoulders and does a little "happy" dance with his front feet. A happy little "Alvin Shuffle." Then Alvin sneezes a few times. When he is really happy, Alvin sneezes. Sneezes of joy.

Instead of reaching to put breakfast in the cage, Bruce reaches in and takes Alvin out of it.

"This is strange," thinks Alvin. "Maybe he is taking me back to my owner. Maybe today is the day that I finally get to go back home."

Alvin likes this prospect and wags his tail with great joy. Alvin likes Bruce. Bruce smells like dog. Alvin has known some good people in his time, and the one trait that they all have in common is that they smell like dog.

Bruce carries Alvin down the hallway. The hallway containing hundreds of cages, stacked one on top of another on top of another on top of another. The hallway of lost and unwanted dogs. All sizes, shapes and colors. All temperaments and virtues. A veritable cornucopia of souls. The lights are dim. The air is completely still and reeks of excrement. At least there aren't any flies. Fly season starts next week.

Bruce walks with Alvin down the hall. Briskly. Methodically. Pointedly. Purposefully. The dog equivalent of the green mile. The hallway of doom.

Bruce brings Alvin into the euthanasia room. It is sparse with dulled white walls, flickering fluorescent lighting, a cabinet on one side and an old stainless steel table in the center of the room. Ropes and muzzles of various length and girth hang on the wall. Bruce will not need any of these, as Alvin is small and easy-going. Indeed, it almost seems as if Alvin is a willing participant. Bruce puts Alvin on the stainless steel table. Alvin wags his tail and looks around.

"Sorry about this, little guy," offers Bruce, "but you are taking up space, and we've got new dogs coming in every day. I've got to empty out cages for the dogs that we could actually rehome. Ones that aren't old, mangy and half-blind. Nobody wants to adopt a dog like you. They want one that is young and cute. That's what they come in here to get."

Alvin wags his tail and looks up at Bruce.

"Ah, you got me! I'm just messin' with 'ya. Nobody goes to a City Shelter to adopt a dog anymore."

Alvin barks at Bruce. He wants to know where his breakfast is.

"This is the worst part of my job," laments Bruce half-heartedly. It's half-hearted because he honestly thinks this is the worst part of his job. However, Bruce would still prefer killing dogs to being a paralegal. He doesn't like taking a life, but he imagines it's easier than working in a cubicle. He will do it 67,531 more times before he retires.

Alvin continues to wag his tail. Bruce takes off Alvin's collar and tosses it on to the countertop. The collar has a big, red "EUTHANIZE" tag on it. It's going to be put on another dog in just a few minutes.

Bruce loads up a glass syringe with a solution of heavy barbiturates. The "death juice." Bruce does this same exact chore twenty to thirty times a day, so his actions are calculated and swift.

Alvin wags his tail.

"Now stay still, Alvin. In six to twelve seconds you will be asleep, and in under a minute you will be, well, wherever is next for you. Whatever's next for any of us. Now, hold still boy."

Bruce hovers over Alvin and grabs him by his right-front leg. Alvin's right-front leg is ticklish, and he enjoys it immensely. Alvin loves to be tickled. It is one of his favorite activities.

Alvin sneezes with joy. Bruce waits for Alvin to stop sneezing. Alvin stops sneezing. Bruce tightens his grip and is just about to inject Alvin when Ken yells to him from the other end of the hallway of cages.

"Bruce! Bruce! DUDE! Where are ya'? BRUUUUUCCCEEE!!!!"

Bruce does not like to be interrupted when he is holding a loaded syringe.

"I'm back here doing God's work! What do you want, Ken?"

"Where's Alvin?"

Bruce looks out the door of the euthanasia room to see Ken all the way down the hall in front of Alvin's cage, a perplexed expression on his face and his arms up in the air just in case Bruce doesn't understand that he's wondering where Alvin is.

"In about three seconds he is going to be headed to doggie heaven!"

"Wait!" screeches Ken, waving his arms frantically back and forth. "Don't do it! Doxie is here!"

"What?"

"Doxie is out front! He's here to pick up Alvin!"

Bruce shrugs and puts the syringe down on the table of death. He gets paid by the hour. Not by the body.

"Well," Bruce explains, "congratulations. It looks like it's your lucky day, Alvin."

Bruce picks up Alvin with one arm and, together, they leave the room of doom. Bruce has never walked out of that room carrying a living dog before. And he never will again. So, once more, Bruce carries Alvin down the green mile hallway. They walk the gauntlet of unwanted and doomed dogs barking uncontrollably with fear and confusion, but this time, in a much happier direction.

Ken, wearing the same blue city issued jumpsuit that Bruce wears minus his name or title as he is only an assistant, has left Alvin's temporary cage and now stands with Doxie by the front counter in the front room of the dog shelter.

Doxie is an extraordinarily obese white man in his forties. His head is round, very much like a beach ball that's been sitting in the sun for too long. He is balding, and the few thin strands of hair that remain are greasy and smelly from lack of washing. He wears brown, plastic framed glasses from the 1970's that have been broken hundreds of times and subsequently repaired very poorly with a vast array of tape and glue. Doxie's skin is blotchy and pasty, and he is extremely pale. Doxie is wearing sweatpants, sandals, and a stained, white T-shirt that reads "Spay and Neuter Your Pets!" in blue magic marker on the front and "Doxie's Dachshund Rescue" in black magic marker on the back. The T-shirt does not cover all of his belly, and the sweatpants do not cover all of his butt-crack. Normally, something like this would expose Doxie's underwear, but Doxie does not believe in wearing underwear. Doxie believes in going "commando." Doxie considers himself a "commando." A commando always on patrol to rescue dachshunds.

Bruce walks into the front room with Alvin. "Hi Doxie," says Bruce.

"Hi Bruce. Whazz'up, hizzle?"

Doxie likes to use the lingo that the kids use. Even though the kids stopped using this particular lingo decades ago. Although Doxie doesn't even use the lingo in any sort of correct context most of the time, he still feels extremely "hip."

"We expected to see you two days ago, Doxie," says Bruce.

"I know," Doxie replies, inhaling. Doxies turns on his machismo. "I threw my back out bustin' a move. I've been laid up in bed with half a dozen ice packs."

"Oh," is all that Bruce has to say to this. He wants no more explanation than what has just been offered.

"Oh my GOD!! Is this Alvin?!" says Doxie with an almost psychotic glee, noticing Alvin for the first time.

"That's what the tag said on his collar when he was brought in," says Bruce and Ken at the same time.

"Where is his collar?" asks Doxie.

"Ummmm...I don't know. Gone?" says Bruce.

"It doesn't matter," Doxie mumbles dismissively. "He's BEAUTIFUL!"

"Ummm..." murmurs Ken, knowing better than to offer an opinion but unwilling to lie for moral reasons.

"Yeah," offers Bruce, fully willing to lie.

Doxie walks over to Bruce and takes Alvin from him.

"So you say that Alvin's owner died, Bruce? Is that what you said?" says Doxie quickly.

"That's the story that we were given, yes. His previous owner, the one that died, apparently rescued him from a puppy mill in Pennsylvania."

"Damn puppy mills!" says Doxie. Doxie spits in disgust.

"The puppy mill part seems to fit because he's got the scars on his jaw from being wired to the cage and he's got a tattoo on his belly, too," adds Ken.

Doxie turns over Alvin, and, indeed, Alvin's belly reads "140 Fk44." This was Alvin's name at the puppy mill. Before he was rescued, he was just known as a soulless code. As a commodity. Then his new owner changed it to Alvin. Alvin likes "Alvin" better than 140 Fk44.

"Alvin's got some health issues you should know about, Doxie," offers Bruce. "He's nearly blind, has glaucoma, cataracts, he's toothless, and his legs have locked up a bit from arthritis. He doesn't walk too well. Probably because he's got some back stuff going on. And maybe his hips. And it looks like he has some issue going on with his anal glands. You'll probably have to express them a couple of times a week. Or day. I dunno'."

"That's okay," insists Doxie. "No biggie. I will love him just the same. Poor little dog. I'll bet you have had the saddest life. How old is he?"

"We think that he is 17," says Bruce, guessing. Guessing correctly, as it turns out. Alvin just turned 17. His birthday was last week. Sadly, nobody knows this. Not even his old owner. Only Alvin. What he doesn't know is that he's the only survivor from the event 17 years ago. He's the last of his litter. The last of his line.

"Seventeen?" Doxie is flummoxed and flustered. "Oh, goodness. That's," trying to do the math with her chubby fingers, "that's 84 in people years. He's ancient. He's a geriatric! Is he neutered?"

"No," says Bruce.

"Oh no," says Doxie, "That just won't do."

"He's 17," offers Ken. "I don't think that you have anything to worry about."

Doxie pouts. Doxie is obviously not convinced that there's nothing to worry about. Indeed, Doxie knows that if you try hard enough, you can always find something to worry about. Always.

"And all your other dogs are spayed, right?" mentions Bruce, trying to diffuse the situation.

"Uh, the shirt?" says Doxie, pointing to the words on his shirt encouraging people to spay and neuter their pets. "I would be a hypocritical fraud wearing my shirt if I had a dog that wasn't. I don't just talk the talk. I walk it, too. I walk it."

Doxie proudly puffs out his chest so "Spay and Neuter Your Pets" is more prominent in the room. This exposes even more of his bulging white belly.

"Would you like to make an appointment?" asks Ken, not wanting to see any more of Doxie's flesh than he has to.

"How about...," Doxie is thinking hard. The wheels are turning. Well, the wheels are grinding. Slowly. Very slowly. "Next Wednesday afternoon? I could come by after bingo."

"Sure," says Ken, not even looking at the appointment book, fairly certain that Alvin won't even live to see next Wednesday. "Next Wednesday's, like, totally awesome."

"See you then," says Doxie, breathing a heavy sigh of relief.

Alvin wags his tail.

"And remember-" begins Doxie with Bruce and Ken chiming in without missing a beat, "If (you) we get a dachshund, call (me) you first."

"All right," continues Bruce with the unmistakable tone of fatigued boredom. "We will. Bye now."

Doxie clutches Alvin and kisses him hard on the mouth. Alvin wags his tail.

"Come on, baby. I'll take good care of you."

Doxie and Alvin go out the front door of the dog shelter.

Doxie's sandals flap with a slap against his fat feet. Ken and Bruce look at each other.

"Do you think that Doxie can take care of another one?" asks Ken.

"I don't know. I guess it's better than putting him to sleep, and it makes our adoption numbers look better," offers Bruce.

Ken shrugs his shoulders and returns to his task of cleaning up dog poop while Bruce goes back to the task of making dogs fall asleep for the very last time. Bruce thinks about little tiny bars of soap. Ken's mind is vacant. That's how they cope.

CHAPTER II

Doxie walks outside into the sunshine and brisk morning air. His car, an old, rusted, lime-green Yugo with bald tires and heavily worn upholstery, is obviously and patently Doxie's. In addition to the vanity license plate that says "DOXIE," dachshund related bumper stickers cover nearly every square inch of the car. This serves a dual purpose. They identify Doxie's personality, and they also act as patches to keep the car in relatively one piece. On the driver's side door, Doxie has painted "Dachshund Rescue Mobile" with a metallic purple spray paint. He did not do a very good job. It looks like bad graffiti. Because it is. The side-view mirrors are long gone, and the missing rear-view mirror has torn a hole in the glass of the windshield. It hurts his neck and back to look behind him or to the side, so Doxie just assumes no one is beside him or behind him. So far, that method of driving has worked out just fine.

Doxie opens the driver's side door and, with great effort, thrusts his arms across the driver's seat and puts Alvin onto the passenger's seat.

Alvin wags his tail and looks up at Doxie.

With an even greater effort, Doxie struggles to get himself into the car. The steering wheel bends against the pressure created by Doxie's belly. Doxie slides onto the seat, his flesh making a "zip" sound against the rippled layers of silver duct tape that hold it together. The key lives permanently in the ignition. This is not a car that anyone would steal, no matter his or her level of desperation.

Doxie reaches into the glove compartment and retrieves a chocolate candy bar. He opens the wrapper with his teeth and eats most of it in one, giant bite. He saves a tiny piece which he offers to Alvin. Alvin shows no interest, but wags his tail at the offer. Alvin doesn't like chocolate. Unlike most other dogs, he knows that it is bad for him and that too much chocolate could kill him. Doxie shrugs, having rarely been smit by an offer of chocolate, and finishes up the last little bite, licking his fingers with an absolutely obsessive urgency. Doxie throws the candy bar wrapper out the window of the car and sizes up Alvin.

"Well, 'Alvin,' we are going to your new home now," coos a sugar-rushed Doxie. "I have to say, I don't much care for your name. There was a mean boy named Alvin who picked on me when I was little. In the winter time, he would make snowballs and put rocks in the center of them and then throw them at my head. In the summer, he would just throw rocks. I had to get stitches on more than one occasion. He terrorized me from pre-school through high school. 16 dreadful years. I think that he is in prison now, for beating up his wife, but they'll let him out someday. He'll be free to terrorize again. I wake up all the time in the middle of the night, in a cold sweat, thinking about this prospect; Alvin freely roaming the streets, stalking me, with snowballs and rocks. So, you see, 'Alvin' will not do. From now on, I'm going to call you...Orville 17!"

Alvin barks and wags his tail at Doxie's enthusiasm. Doxie is happy that Alvin is happy.

"Yes! Orville 17! Let's go home, boy."

Doxie turns the key and the engine whirs. He turns the key again and it groans. He turns the key a third time and it both whirs and groans. On the fourth time, the car starts. Doxie throws the gear shift into "drive" and pulls out of the parking lot.

Doxie is what could be referred to as an "aggressive" driver.

Without mirrors, Doxie is rather oblivious to any dangers on the road that are not right in front of him. That is just fine with Doxie. Driving a car, just like every other thing in his life, is guided by pure, instinctive tunnel-vision. If it is not right in front of him, it does not count and he doesn't give a damn.

Doxie just picks a lane and punches the gas. He's a rebel.

Fighting for another candy bar in the glove box, Doxie doesn't notice being nearly side-swiped by a shiny, black Mercedes as he careens past the flower shop on Main Street. Doxie just keeps driving, not knowing how close he just came to getting into what could have been a very serious accident.

The Mercedes blazes on down the road and, without signaling, cuts in front of an old Dodge K-car, a brown wreck with faded purple pin stripes that belongs to a worker-bee named Trent. In only eleven more payments, the car will be paid for. Trent slams on his brakes to avoid hitting the Mercedes and blows a tire and loses control of the steering. Trent's car comes screeching to a halt, slamming up against the curb of the sidewalk. Suddenly and simultaneously, the radiator explodes and the head gasket fails. Trent shakes his fist in the air. Trent gets out of his steaming, smoking car to survey the damage. There is a lot. Trent will be late for work, for sure.

Doxie drives by, oblivious to the situation. Trent tries to get Doxie's attention by waving him down in a frantic attempt to get a ride in to work, but Doxie is too busy eating chocolate and staring directly at the road in front of himself to notice. Trent is left standing alone on the side of the road.

Trent feels both angry and sad. These emotions are not new to him. They're the story of Trent's life. They cloak him daily.

Doxie drives as fast as his little car will take them. Every three blocks or so, he reaches with great difficulty over to the glove compartment and pulls out another chocolate candy bar. When he does, the steering wheel turns to the left, forced by his belly, and he has to compensate by steering hard to the right. Doxie opens the candy bar wrapper with his teeth, eats the vast majority of it with one bite, and throws the wrapper out the window. Again he offers a piece the size of a pinkie nail to Alvin. Alvin always politely refuses. Doxie eats the last little bit and licks his fingers clean, all the while weaving in and out of traffic and zooming around corners. Alvin is tossed around a bit, but doesn't really care. He thinks it's kind of fun.

Doxie makes a sharp left turn into one of the more run-down parts of town. The houses are small, one story, prefab jobs that were built at the end of World War II. Most still sport what is left of the original lead-based paint. All are in need of new roofing material, and the small lots they sit on are littered with dead trees and dead shrubs sitting in the middle of dirt that, 30 years ago, used to support all sorts of life and hope for the future in the form of a lawn.

Doxie passes an empty lot. Empty being a relative term. The lot does not have a house on it, but it is filled with junk. A lot of junk. Three 17-year-old young adults stand in the middle of the lot. Doobie, Moonbeam, and Socrates. Their hair is long and they exude the essence of "Freak Power." Doobie, Moonbeam and Socrates each hold four, 50-gallon capacity black plastic trash bags. They just got to the lot a few minutes ago and the engine of their VW bus is still warm. They are contemplating all of the work that needs to be done. The 600 gallons of trash they can pick up won't make a dent in what it will take to reclaim this little spot of Mother Earth, but they know it needs to be done. She's worth it.

Doobie, Moonbeam and Socrates each wear home-made tie-dye shirts, jeans with holes in them, and sandals. Every inch of their clothing, right down to their underwear, is made of hemp. Except for Moonbeam. He doesn't believe in wearing underwear. If Moonbeam and Doxie knew each other, they could start a club. Moonbeam finds underwear to be too restricting beneath his tight pants. Moonbeam disagrees with "restricting" on practically every level. Almost all forms of restriction give him an upset stomach, diarrhea, and a bad case of hives on his chest and legs. The real reason Moonbeam doesn't wear any underwear is because he is very poor and can't afford to buy any. So he doesn't.

Socrates' tie-dye T-shirt reads "Will Work For Love." And he means it. He bought it for twenty-five cents at one of the local thrift stores. No one has ever taken him up on the offer, and he has worn the shirt every day for the past five months. He is sure that someone, someday, will respond to it. When they do, the price of the shirt will have paid for itself in spades. He might get more of a response to the shirt if he would ever wash it, but Socrates has never considered this.

Doobie, Socrates and Moonbeam call themselves the "Righteous Recyclers." They spend their days picking up trash and recycling everything that they can. Plastic, paper, aluminum, steel, glass and cardboard. They do it for themselves. They do it for their neighbor. They do it for humanity. They do it for Mother Earth. Mostly, they do it to avoid getting a job that involves any kind of supervision. They don't ever want to have to work for "The Man." That would mean having to "sell out." They made a pact, long ago, never to "sell out" to "The Man." Ever.

They have been recycling for ten weeks now, and have been averaging an income of five dollars each. Per day. They get paid by the pound, and they like to take lots of breaks. But they all agree that it still beats working for "The Man." And it is.

They are the only hippies in Midland City under the age of 40. When they bothered to go to high school, they never fell into the punk, goth, rap, metal, new-wave, new-age, country, country/western, western, blues, preppie, hip-hop, grunge, jock, band geek or nerd thing. They are "granola." They fell in love with love, and they fell in love with the 1960's, and that is how they are living their lives. Their core values are generations in the past. And now, here, they have made those core values the seed for living in the present that will eventually grow into the future. The growth is slow.

"There sure is a lot of stuff here," says Moonbeam.

"I'll bet we can recycle most of it," adds Doobie.

"Look," says Socrates, "there are three staples. Over there by the empty pizza box. We can recycle those."

"Good eye," congratulates Moonbeam.

"Let's get to work," says Doobie with mild inspiration.

They get to work. Socrates goes right for the three staples and puts them in one of the fifty gallon bags, a huge, self-satisfied smile on his face. Moonbeam pats him on the back. Doobie, Moonbeam and Socrates all smile and nod their heads. They are well on their way to earning their five dollars each.

The Righteous Recyclers are straight-edge hippies, meaning that they don't believe in drugs or alcohol. And that pretty much totally sucks because drugs and alcohol would make their job a LOT more fun. Or, at least tolerable. But they are young men of standards and strong belief and high moral character, so they will not resort to introducing chemicals in to their otherwise chaste bodies. Besides, if they did, they would kill the single brain cell that they have left between them. Then where would they be?

Doxie, however, pays no mind to the cleaners of Mother Earth and makes a sharp left turn and speeds down the middle of the street to the end of the block. Doxie makes another left, then a right. The car races down the street and Doxie makes another right hand turn, flying to the middle of the block. The car screeches to a halt in front of Doxie's small, disheveled house. Just like every other house, the front yard is unkempt and the lawn is long, long gone. The only life in the yard are weeds growing up between cracks in the cement porch. They have a fairly brownish hue, so they pretty much look dead, anyway.

What was once white paint peels off the exterior of the house, and the roof is in desperate need of shingles. All of the blinds and curtains are drawn. The home looks totally unoccupied. That's how Doxie wants it. He wants to be incognito. Stay under the radar.

Doxie slams the car into park and turns off the engine.

The engine sputters and knocks, but finally stops running. The neighborhood is completely silent. Not even a single bird can be heard chirping. This part of town is too poor for birds.

He opens the door. With great effort, he struggles to extricate himself from the front seat. When he is nearly out, he reaches over and grabs Alvin. Alvin wags his tail.

Doxie slams the car door and waddles up the front path of dirt to the porch and takes a key out of his pocket. The key is on a yellow piece of yarn, the same yellow piece of yarn that's been attached to it since Doxie was in third grade. He was a latchkey child. Doxie puts the key in the lock and turns it. He opens the front door.

The second the door is open a mere tiny crack, 200 dachshunds suddenly bark as if the world is about to end. The sound is deafening.

Doxie opens the door the rest of the way, pushing dogs away with the sweeping motion of the door. Masses of dachshunds besiege Doxie when he is finally able to enter the house. Doxie closes the door behind him and carefully locks it.

Doxie's house is beyond filthy. It is a health hazard. A small sofa and coffee table lay on their respective sides in the unused living room. A thick layer of poop and urine cover the floor and walls. Although, to be fair to the dogs, some of the poop and urine is Doxie's.

Sometimes, especially late at night, he just doesn't feel like walking the ten feet to the bathroom. It would just take too much of an effort. And something bad could happen. Like he could stub his toe in the dark. Nope. Too risky.

The carpet is stained and embedded with filth to the point that maggots now infest it. It is crusty and gives off an odor that has caused the paint to peel off the walls. The plywood underneath the carpet has become so super-saturated with excrement that it is warped and bowed and the wood fibers have been replaced with excrement fibers. Several weak spots will soon give way under the pressure of Doxie's immense weight. Someday, someday soon, Doxie will fall through the floor into the crawl-space. He will become stuck. He will panic. He will have a massive heart-attack. He will die there. He will die there, and the dogs will eat him.

But not today.

For now, it is business as usual at Doxie's house. Doxie flips on the light. It is an old floor lamp that he found in the trash in an alley many years ago. It has an electrical short, and only works half the time.

No pictures adorn the walls.

Doxie keeps the curtains drawn at all times to prevent the curious stares of neighbors. Not that the neighbors would care. Everyone in this part of town is so poor, disheartened, depressed and paranoid that caring is out of their realm. They can't even care for themselves, let alone anyone else. That's okay with Doxie. He likes his privacy. He has to be careful. By law, he's only allowed to keep four dogs in his house because he lives in a residential neighborhood. Doxie is pretty sure that he has more than that. He's pretty sure that, no matter what, nobody is taking any of them away from him. Ever.

Stacks of newspapers line the walls of his living room. Doxie used to lay them on the floor for the dog mess, and they are still under there because he never got around to picking them up. He just puts a new layer on top of the messy old layer. There is over ten years of newspaper covering the floor. It is somewhat of a horror show, but it is Doxie's horror show, so he's pretty used to it by now.

"Hello my babies!" screeches Doxie, pitching into his usual 'I am home' routine. "Hello Franny 11 and 8! Hello Hershey 5 through 12! Hello Zelda 6! Hello, babies! Everyone, we have a new addition to our happy family! Let me introduce you to...Orville 17!"

Doxie has only 10 names for his dogs. He only likes 10 names in all of the languages in all of the world. He feels that only 10 names are dog-worthy. This was not an issue with him until he got his 11th dog. So now he gives them a number after their names so that he can tell them apart.

Doxie puts Alvin on the floor.

"Look! Orville 16, meet Orville 17!"

Doxie nudges Orville 16 towards Alvin, but Orville 16 is not interested. Zelda 12, however, sniffs Alvin's butt. Alvin likes this.

"Is everybody ready for lunch?"

The dogs bark even more furiously, having heard the "L" word. Doxie serves five meals a day to his dogs. The 10a.m. feeding is called lunch, which naturally comes after breakfast. Afternoon snack is at 1p.m., dinner is at 3p.m., evening snack comes at 7p.m. and then that's it for the day. There is a routine at Doxie's house, and you can set your watch by it. The dogs know this. They certainly set theirs. Their internal clocks are as precise as any finely man-made Swiss timepiece sold in the finest of stores for tens of thousands of dollars.

Doxie wanders into the kitchen. Alvin, and all the other dogs, follow him. Doxie opens up the refrigerator door and peers inside. He pauses a minute to survey the contents, which is strange, because the only food in the refrigerator are 100 count boxes of hot dogs and individual cans of Tab soda. It's not like he is planning to feed the dogs Tab. He already tried this once, and it was a miserable failure. It just made the dogs throw up. Instantly. In projectile fashion. All over the floors and walls. Doxie was planning on cleaning it up. Just like he planned to pick up the newspapers after the dogs pooped and peed on them. Many years ago. Alas, he never quite got around to it. He's not going to start now. He can't. It's lunchtime.

Someday, though. Someday.

At least, that's what he tells himself every night right before bedtime. He's really good at giving himself pep-talks right before he falls asleep. He has a problem remembering them upon awakening, though. That's why his life is stuck in such a rut and nothing ever changes.

Doxie stares intensely into the refrigerator. After a minute or so, he reaches in and takes out one of the boxes of hot dogs. He rips open the top of the box and pours the contents on the floor. It quickly becomes a feeding-frenzy.

Doxie spies Alvin, standing off by himself, wagging his tail, not partaking in the meal.

"Orville 17, don't you like hot dogs?"

Alvin wags his tail. Doxie stares intensely at Alvin, trying to get into Alvin's mind. To connect their two brains together. To communicate. To understand. To fuse into "one." To know each other's greatest hopes and fears and plans for the future; the future and beyond. Before Doxie has time to interpret Alvin's personality and character, a voice comes bellowing in from the back bedroom. The voice belongs to an old woman.

"Doxie! Doxie, is that you? Doxie?"

"Yes, Mommy," Doxie replies with a noticeable degree of measured impatience.

"Get in here, boy!" counters Mommy, with a noticeable degree of not-so-measured impatience.

Doxie begrudgingly steps over the feasting dogs, picks up Alvin, and heads back into Mommy's room. He knows what awaits him. It is "The Talk." The very same "Talk" that they have had countless times. At least a hundred million times. Doxie is sick of it, but it is the price he has to pay to live here. He doesn't have to pay rent, but he has to suffer through "The Talk." In Doxie's mind, suffering through "The Talk" counts as his rent. And his share of utilities. And food. And clothing. But, wow, "The Talk" sure sucks.

Doxie walks down the short hallway and into Mommy's bedroom.

Mommy is a bed-ridden, old, frail, black woman with white, curly hair and thick, thick eyeglasses. Her eyeballs look the size of silver dollars behind the thick glass. Empty cans of Tab soda are strewn about the room, and dozens of ashtrays overflow with cigarette butts. Mommy wears a pristine, white nightgown and is smoking two cigarettes at once. Ornate, lace-fringed quilts cover her emaciated, frail, old legs.

Mommy's room is dark and dank. Shelves line every inch of the walls. On the shelves are a vast array of containers. Ornate wooden boxes, ceramic bowls, and clay jars. Their initial intended purpose long gone, they now serve a greater need.

When someone with no family dies, whether they be destitute or otherwise alone, they are cremated at no charge by the fine people at the Coroner's Office for the City and County of Midland. The City Coroner (Jimbo the Coroner, as he's known to his friends) keeps the ashes for two years and, if by that time, no one has claimed them, they are disposed of. The website for the Midland City Coroner's Office insinuates that the unclaimed ashes are sprinkled in the middle of the park on a beautiful summer's day, but the truth of the matter is that Jimbo the Coroner is extremely lazy and has bad allergies, so the ashes wind up in a cardboard box in the dumpster behind the crematorium, which is where Doxie's Mom retrieved them.

Doxie's Mommy learned about the practice of disposing the unclaimed ashes in the dumpster thirty-years ago. Back then, she would love to go crawling around in dumpsters. Dumpster diving was her hobby. Partially because of the practicality of being a single mother on a limited income, and partially because she thought that it was a lot of fun. It was like a treasure hunt. She would be amazed at what some people would throw away. Clothes, electronics, furniture. Even money.

One day, she was dumpster diving downtown and stumbled upon the cremated ashes of Bob Smith in a clear, plastic baggie. She knew that it was Bob Smith because it was labeled "Cremated ashes of Bob Smith" in neat, black lettering. She thought that a dumpster was no place for the physical remnants of a human being, so she took them home, emptied out her jewelry box onto her dresser and put the plastic baggie of ashes into it. Later, she would find more plastic baggies of ashes, take them home, and find an appropriate storage container for them. This went on for quite some time.

Doxie's Mommy got caught digging in the dumpster one day and Jimbo the Coroner made a deal with her that if she didn't tell anyone that he has been throwing out the ashes, she could come claim them. In the office, without climbing into the dumpster. She agreed. However, since her legs had failed and she had become bed-ridden almost 20-

years ago, the coroner just calls her on the phone and she has Doxie go down and pick them up.

Doxie's Mommy claims the forgotten ones. The unwanted souls. The un-remembered. Until Doxie's Mommy gives them a "forever" home.

Doxie's Mommy loves her hobby, but is less thrilled with Doxie's. She feels that they are both doing a good thing, but the forgotten ones and the un-remembered ashes don't need to be fed. They don't bark. In fact, they don't make any noise at all. They don't poop and pee all over her house and make it smell bad. They just slumber in a container on a shelf. No fuss, no muss.

"What do you want, Mommy?"

Doxie knows exactly what Mommy wants.

"Doxie, when are you gonna' clean up after them dogs?"

"I can't right now, Mommy. I have to get ready for my gig tonight."

Doxie is impatient and shifts Alvin from one arm to the other. Mommy is also impatient and takes alternate drags off each of her double-fisted cigarettes.

"What's this 'gig' you keep talkin' about, boy?"

"I told you, Mommy. Like, about a hundred times, I've told you. I have this big gig tonight! It's important!"

Mommy hates to hear this.

"Why don't you just give up this rock 'n roll dream of yours, boy? Get a job. Get a woman. Or a man. I don't care. Just move out. Move out and take all them dogs with you!"

"I can't give up my dream, Mommy! You know that I got rock 'n roll in my blood! It's impossible to deny it! What am I supposed to do?"

Mommy's heart is about to break. She already knows the answer to his question, and he knows that she knows and he asked it anyway. It is part of their routine. It is a part of "The Talk."

"I know. You're sick with it, boy. Ain't nothin' you can do."

"It's God's gift to me, Mommy! You know it just as well as I do! The Rock and Roll is GOD'S GIFT an' it's all I got!!!"

"I know that, boy. I know. You can't do nothin' 'bout a gift from God."

"I wouldn't have it in my blood if my Daddy wasn't Elvis!"

Immediately, Doxie regretted saying those words. He shouldn't have brought it up. He didn't mean to bring it up. It just sort of slipped out. Mommy was pretty upset before, but now Mommy is on the verge of totally losing it. It escalates to this extreme every few weeks.

"Elvis warned me, after he got me pregnant with you, that this would happen!" is all that Mommy can barely choke out of her mouth.

And then Mommy loses it. She begins to cry furiously. Doxie shuffles his feet.

"He warned me!" Mommy sobs. Mommy shakes like she's having a seizure, but her eyeglasses stay perfectly in place.

"Don't blame yourself, Mommy!" Doxie hates it when Mommy blames herself. "I'm glad my Daddy is Elvis. It's a gift! It's all a gift!"

"I know, boy. I know."

Mommy's lie to Doxie so many years ago, about being the illegitimate son of Elvis, has been told and re-told so many times between the two of them that she now believes the lie herself. The lie began as an answer to why Doxie is white, and Mommy is black. It was certainly a valid question. So many years have gone by now that the truthful answer is lost. Doxie's Mommy has no idea how in the hell she wound up with a white son. Maybe he's the son of Elvis. Or maybe he's the son of the assistant night manager at Jack In The Box. But none of this matters any more. The lie is now all the truth there is. Or needs to be. Or ever will be. It has a life of its own, and it will outlive all of us.

Mommy tries to calm herself with smoking. It sort of works. Kind of. Mommy looks over at the clock.

"God's Nightgown!" shouts Mommy with such an overabundance of panicked tone and inflection that you'd think she'd just realized that a king cobra was slithering up her leg.

"What, Mommy?"

"It's time for my show! Turn on the TV, Doxie! Turn it on!"

Doxie goes to the foot of Mommy's bed to the television and turns on the only knob that is still connected. The old, small, black and white comes to life and the sound pops on with a sharp *CRACK* just as the "Moises McSweeney Joy Love Hour" is beginning. The "I've Got the Joy in My Heart" theme music plays, and Moises can be heard singing the tune.

"Oh, heavens! I almost missed it! Now be a good son and go get your Mommy a Tab."

"Okay Mommy."

"The Talk" is officially over. Doxie walks back to the kitchen with Alvin, stepping over numerous Orvilles and Hersheys and Zeldas and Frannys. Alvin wags his tail. Doxie puts Alvin down on the kitchen floor. All of the hot dogs have been eaten.

"Now you be good, Orville 17. I don't want to have any trouble from you."

Alvin wags his tail.

"Where's my Tab, boy!?" yells Mommy from her bedroom.

"Coming, Mommy!" Doxie looks at Alvin. "Mommy is almost at her wit's end."

Doxie picks up Alvin and opens the door to the back yard. Numerous dachshunds roam outside in the yard.

"You should probably just stay out here for the morning so you don't bother Mommy. Here," he says, putting Alvin down on the parched dirt, "enjoy the sunshine. Enjoy the fresh air. Enjoy your new life, Orville 17!"

"Doxie!" bellows Mommy.

"Coming, Mommy!"

Doxie closes the door to the back yard. Alvin looks back at the door and wags his tail. Alvin waits. He is a very patient dog.

CHAPTER III

After a few hours, Alvin realizes that Doxie
may not be coming back any time soon. He decides
it might be fun to explore the yard. As he quickly
discovers, there is not much to explore. It is plain
and flat with some twigs sticking out of the ground
that may or may not represent where some shrubs
used to be. There are no trees. It doesn't look like
there ever have been. The dirt has been baked as
solid as concrete, and it all looks just like a barren,
lunar landscape. Except for the copious amounts of
dog poop and urine stains that cake the dirt. So it
more resembles a lunar landscape that was a dog
park for a hundred years and nobody ever bothered
to clean it up. Ever.

Two dogs come up to greet Alvin. Well, one
greets him, and the other one just kind of runs in to
him, but Alvin considers it a greeting. Their names
are Simon 11 and Edgar 9.

Simon 11 is all black with a wee bit of white
around his eyes and mouth. He had a good home
with a loving family, but they moved far away and
couldn't take him with them. Well, they could have
taken him with them, but it wouldn't have been

convenient. In these modern times, life is all about convenience. So he got dumped at the Midland City Dog Shelter, entrusted to the pathos of Bruce and Ken. Simon 11 is a happy dog and loves to play fetch, but he has nothing to play fetch with. He misses his family dearly. So now he just wanders around Doxie's backyard and waits to die.

Edgar 9, on the other hand, suffers from severe dementia. He is the one that ran into Alvin. Edgar 9 is tan and white with wiry fur, completely blind and deaf and walks around in circles all day long. Clockwise. The moment he wakes up in the morning, he jumps to his feet and turns to the right and walks really, really fast. He does this all day long. Edgar 9 forgets things. Like walking straight or turning to the left. Sometimes, Edgar 9 forgets to eat and drink water. He doesn't care, though. He is happy just walking in circles. It is his short term goal and his long term goal and he achieves it every few seconds. For Edgar 9, it's all good.

Simon 11 wants to play fetch with Alvin, or anyone for that matter, but he sees that Alvin doesn't have anything to play fetch with, so Simon 11 walks away. He will just sit in a corner of the yard and think about what his life used to be like as he dies slowly on the inside. Edgar 9 walks away, too. Then he comes back. Then away again. Then back. Then away. His actions make Alvin dizzy.

All the other dogs ignore Alvin, but he still feels welcome. Well, maybe not "welcome," but he doesn't feel "unwelcome." He doesn't feel like he's in any danger or anything like that. He can be himself and not be judged. He begins to walk the perimeter of the yard in his own stilted, slow fashion, lifting his paws high and walking in full, arthritis-racked steps. Alvin discovers a small hole in the fence that leads to the neighbor's yard. The hole is just big enough for Alvin to squeeze through. Feeling adventurous, Alvin squeezes through the hole and enters the neighbor's yard.

The neighbor's yard is also empty. Almost. It is empty except for Spike and Butch; two mammoth black and tan Rottweilers with huge, pointy teeth. They charge at Alvin, mouths frothing with a demonic look in their eyes. Alvin wags his tail. Spike and Butch stop dead in their tracks. They sniff Alvin.

Spike sniffs Alvin's face and Butch sniffs Alvin's butt. Alvin feels popular. Alvin continues to wag his tail. Soon they all wag their tails. Spike and Butch like Alvin. They like his "vibe." And Alvin likes them. Spike and Butch soon lose interest in Alvin and run through a doggie door that leads into the kitchen of the house. Alvin slowly follows them through the door gleefully, wagging his tail the whole time. Alvin is always thrilled to make new friends.

What Alvin sees as he enters the house, even with his poor eyesight, is something that he has never seen before. That is only because Alvin has never seen anyone cooking up methamphetamine before. The kitchen of the neighbor's house is exactly like Doxie's house (minus the dogs, poop and urine issues) but is filled with all sorts of industrial laboratory equipment. Beakers and bottles and Bunsen burners and stirrers. Shane and Jim, Doxie's neighbors, are really, really, really busy.

Shane is a man of medium build with several "prison" tattoos on his arms. He calls them prison tattoos, but he has never actually been to prison. The man who did them just used cheap ink and did a bad job. It is a lot cooler to say that you got your tattoos in prison than to confess that you just used incredibly poor judgment and had them done by a total moron. Repeatedly.

Shane's long brown hair is pulled back in a ponytail, covering the back of his "Kip Winger World Tour" T-shirt. His pockmarked face shows little expression, other than annoyance at the fact that he has the hiccups. Shane doesn't know why he has the hiccups. They just started this morning, and they are relentless. It could be allergies. Or a summer cold. Or nerves. Or all of the above. He doesn't know. All he knows for certain is that they are starting to bug the hell out of him. He's worried that if anybody sees him like this, he will lose his "street cred." Street cred that he never had to begin with because he wears Kip Winger World Tour T-shirts, has crappy tattoos and wears his hair pulled back in a ponytail.

Jim, on the other hand, looks a bit like Albert Einstein on crack. A very well-tanned Albert Einstein on crack. His hair is messy and his white cotton shirttail is half tucked in and half un-tucked. He wears black pants and an old pair of beat up brown Converse high top shoes with numerous holes in them. Jim actually has a lot of street cred. He doesn't care.

Jim is the brains of the outfit, and Shane has ridden on his coattails for almost three months now. They met in the Midland City Jail. Shane was doing time for breaking a man's legs in a bar fight, and Jim was in trouble for stalking a woman that he'd never even met or talked to. Jim was good at stalking. Very calculating and efficient and proficient. He had boxes filled with pictures, voice recordings from illegal wire-taps, and various undergarments that belonged to the woman that he was far too preoccupied with.

Her name was Lucy. Lucy Snodderly. He saw her on the bus. She was sitting in the front seat with her groceries, and Jim was sitting in the middle of the bus. Jim was on his way to a court mandated Alcoholics Anonymous meeting. Jim saw Lucy and, for some unknown rational reason, something in Jim's brain told him that he had to know everything

about her. Every intimate detail. Without actually
meeting her. Ever since Jim stopped drinking
alcohol, he found it impossible to talk to women.
He was just too nervous and too shy. So his sober
brain told him that his only option was to stalk her.
Jim had never tried stalking before, and he was
amazed at how easy it was. He was also amazed at
how easy breaking and entering her apartment was
while she was not home. He was amazed at how
easy it was to steal her panties and her bras without
her knowing. Just one per visit, so that she would
not know that they were gone. Jim had never really
been good at anything his entire life, but all of this,
he mastered almost instantly. He was finally good at
something. He broke in to her apartment 17 times
until he was caught by an alert neighbor who also
happened to be far too preoccupied with the
woman. Then it was over. Once you get caught, it is
widely considered that you have failed at your
particular crime. He was officially no longer good at
anything.

While in jail, Jim and Shane became close
friends, as they shared a 6-foot by 10-foot piece of
barred real estate together for 16 hours a day. After
agreeing not to rape each other or draw on each
other's face with permanent marker while they
slept, they soon settled into a routine of playing
cards and sharing stories and lies about their lives to
pass the time.

One day, while having lunch in the cafeteria, they met Scully.

Scully was doing time for shoplifting. Scully shoplifted a car. So his crime was more commonly known as auto theft. Although Scully explained to the judge that he was only borrowing the car to drive his sick grandmother to church on Sunday and had every intention of returning it, the judge did not believe him. Mostly because the car was taken on a Tuesday and Scully's grandmother has been dead for 20 years. The mob then bought off the judge, so Scully only got sentenced to six months in jail. With time off for good behavior and for time served and for bribes given to the district attorney, two more judges and a Texas Marshal, Scully was to serve a grand total of three days in jail. If the police discovered that there was a dead body stuffed in the framework of the car, Scully would have served a lot more time. Maybe. But probably not. The mob has deep pockets and there are a lot of people who hold high positions of power who are really, really greedy.

While eating their institutionally prepared hamburgers and french fries, Scully inquired as to what Jim and Shane were planning on doing upon their release. Shane planned on finding the man's legs that he broke and break them again for pressing charges against him. Maybe he might break the man's neck for good measure. Jim was planning to find someone new to stalk. He was finally over

Lucy, but his life felt like there was a void in it. A huge void that needed to be filled. He really enjoyed stalking. He knew that he'd do better at it this time, now that he'd had some practice. And also because stalking was more rewarding than teaching science at the Midland City Junior Community College. But Scully had a much more interesting proposition for them both.

"How would you boys like to make some money? REAL money?" inquired Scully.

Well, neither Jim nor Shane had ever made REAL money before. You know, REAL money. Not only the kind of money that is substantially more than minimum wage, but also the kind of money that you probably don't want to try to report to the government when tax time rolls around. Shane and Jim were interested. This was all Scully needed to hear. He knew the Mob was in the market for a chemist and some muscle and he got both of those. So, upon their release, Jim and Shane found themselves gainfully employed by the Midland City Mafia with a nice salary and health and dental benefits available after 90 days of employment. It felt good to have a job.

Jim wasn't sure if he could tolerate Shane after they got out of jail, but they have gotten along perfectly since then. The only issue that they have with each other is whether the toilet paper in the bathroom should unroll in an "over" fashion, or an "under" fashion. This was not an issue while they were in jail, as the toilet paper came out of an institutional dispenser and there was only one way for it to come out. Straight. Now they are back on the outside, where toilet paper rolls freely. Shane insists that it should feed out in an overly fashion, as that is how it was when he was growing up, but Jim insists that it should feed out in an underly fashion, as was the wont of his youth. The toilet paper gets shifted daily.

One thing that they can both agree on, however, is that the toilet itself is seriously messed up. It being a rental home, and the owner living in a different state, some haphazard plumbing work was done on it about a year and a half ago. The pipes had burst during a particularly cold stretch during a particularly cold winter and needed to be replaced. The plumber, who happened to be a friend of the homeowner's brother, had bet 250 dollars on a baseball game being played the very night the pipes burst. Naturally, the plumber didn't care too much about work and wanted to go to a bar to watch the game on TV. Well, not just a bar, but his favorite bar. A bar where everyone knows his name. But they don't know it in a good way. They know his name because he's a raging alcoholic loudmouth know-it-all who makes a fool out of himself on a regular basis.

The clock was ticking closer and closer to game time and he was almost finished with the job when he ran out of materials and the hardware store was on the other end of town. The plumber started freaking out. If there was ever a game that he was more certain he could ruin for everyone by being a loudmouth obnoxious jerk, it was the game tonight. And he needed a drink. Bad. His hands were starting to shake.

After some creative problem-solving, he determined that he could finish the job right then if he ran the hot water pipe into the bathroom toilet. So he did. He went to the bar where everyone knows his name and watched the game. He drank. He cheered and yelled. He drank. He drank and drank and drank. He lost 250 dollars. He got arrested on the way home for driving drunk. And then he hung himself in jail. As far as the landlord is concerned, since his brother's friend is dead and he didn't know any other cheap plumbers, the toilet has water and it flushes so the toilet is officially fixed and there's nothing else to discuss about it. So now the toilet steams for quite some time after it has been flushed. Sometimes it just steams on its own. Nobody reads the Sunday newspaper on this toilet. No way. Jim and Shane make quick use of it when they need to. After switching the roll of toilet paper around, of course.

Now it is crunch time for Shane and Jim. There's no time to think about toilets or toilet paper. They are really, really busy and really, really focused. And they are nervous. Very, very nervous.

When Spike and Butch come tearing through the kitchen, they are less than pleased.

"Look out!" freaks Jim. "Stupid dogs! They're gonna' send this place sky-high if they knock over one of the burners."

"It's not," hiccups Shane, "the dogs' fault. You should have locked the doggie door." Shane hiccups. "That's what you should have done."

Alvin saunters into the kitchen. He is wagging his tail.

"Whoa!" exclaims Jim. "Look! It's a wiener dog from next door!"

"Spike!" Shane hiccups. "Butch!" And he hiccups again. "Why didn't you eat him?"

Alvin looks up at Shane and wags his tail. Spike and Butch wag their tails. Ignorant to the respect that Spike and Butch afford Alvin, Jim thinks he has the answer.

"They must be full from the four that they ate this morning."

Butch and Spike don't like to eat Doxie's dachshunds. They only do it because Jim and Shane feed them sub-par dog food. Butch and Spike have high standards. If they are going to eat dog meat, it should at least be fresh.

"Do you think," Shane hiccups, painfully, "that freakin' fat idiot next door has noticed that," gulping another painful hiccup, "his dogs have been disappearing for the past three," extremely painful hiccup, "weeks?"

"Apparently not," says Jim.

"Is that batch almost done?" Shane hiccups.

"Almost. Bags packed?"

"Yes. Clothes in the blue bag and," not-so-painful hiccup, "57 pounds of meth in the black bag." Semi-painful hiccup. "I'm nervous about this, dude." Mild hiccup. "When the mob finds out that we are taking the drugs and skipping-" painful hiccup, "town, they are going to want to kill-" extremely painful hiccup, "us."

"Don't worry. They won't be able to find us. We'll rent a car, drive the stuff down to Bobby in Texas, he will pay us in cash and platinum, and then we fly to Costa Rica. The mob will never find us in Costa Rica."

"Why don't we just sell the stuff to the," hiccup, "Mob?"

"Because we can make a LOT more money this way. We can retire. We'll never have to work another day in our lives. It will be just like winning the lottery. Without the taxes."

"Well I'm," hiccup, "nervous."

"And you should see a doctor about those hiccups."

"I'll see a doctor," hiccup, "in Costa Rica." Then Shane has a very painful, debilitating hiccup that almost knocks him over.

The doorbell rings. Jim and Shane look at each other with fearful anticipation. Shane hiccups. The doorbell rings again.

"I'll get it," says Jim, finally.

Jim goes to the front door as Shane clutches the black suitcase, ready to run out the back door if necessary. Jim looks out the security peephole on the front door.

"It's okay," he yells back to the kitchen. "It's just a couple of bums. I'll get rid of 'em."

Jim opens the front door. Before him stand George and Ralph.

George and Ralph wear mismatched shoes and their ill-fitting jeans have stains all over them from continuous use. Ralph's shirt used to be blue, and George's shirt used to be green, but the sun and the weather took-care of that. Now they are simply an institutional grey. George is only wearing one sock, as he used the other one to contain the blood-flow on Ralph's head when Ralph got hit in the head last week by a flying object and wound up having to throw it away.

The gash to Ralph's head was an accident. It was a freak Frisbee accident in the park. The accident was caused by Doobie, Socrates and Moonbeam, celebrating a successful day of saving Mother Earth by playing Frisbee in the park. The hippie teens were so sorry that they gave George and Ralph 15 dollars, their entire days' wages, for having to go through all the trouble of bleeding and then having to waste a sock and then pollute Mother Earth by sending it to a landfill.

Ralph and George have matching beards and they are both missing exactly the opposite teeth. Ralph would always tell George, "If you could blend our two mouths together we could eat a steak for dinner." George never understood what he meant by that.

George is wearing an old ball-cap with "I laughed, I cried, it was better than Cats" on the front of it. George found the hat blowing down the sidewalk during a really nasty wind storm. He had to run almost two blocks to catch up with it. And, once he saw what the hat said, he was glad that he had put in the effort to obtain it. George doesn't like cats, as he believes them to be insolent beasts from hell, so he wears the hat with great pride. In his eyes, EVERYTHING is better than cats. George doesn't know that *Cats* is a Broadway musical play with people.

Ralph could hear Jim yell "Bum" and is less than appreciative.

They are not bums. They are men, like all other men. They have thoughts and opinions and fears and feelings. They just don't have a home. They could have a home, but that costs money, and they don't have any of that. Which is why they are going door to door in Midland City right now.

"What do you want?" asks Jim with the patience of a man who is about to smuggle and sell over 50 pounds of crystal methamphetamine and flee the country from the Mob.

"Good morning sir," says Ralph, for the 20th time today. "Please allow me to introduce ourselves. My name is Ralph and this is George."

"Hello," says George, politely removing his hat.

"What do you want?" says Jim again, looking back towards the kitchen.

"We are collecting today for a charity," continues Ralph.

"For The Bearded Clams of Madagascar," interrupts George. Ralph buries his face in his hands.

"What the hell are you talking about?" says Jim, more than a little shocked.

"We need to save the Bearded Clams of Madagascar," says George in earnest. "Or they will die out and there will be no more of them forever and the little children will never be able to see them."

"Or we could wash your windows," quickly interjects Ralph.

"Go to hell," says Jim, slamming the door on their faces.

Ralph looks at George. Ralph could yell at George, but he never has and he won't start now. Ralph knows that George isn't playing with a full deck of cards and he is just a little slow and it's not his fault.

"It isn't Georges' fault," Ralph tells himself in his head. "It's just how he was born."

Ralph looks at George. George looks at Ralph.

"Now you see, George," begins Ralph out loud, slowly, just like he did at the last house, and the last house before that, and all of the ones before that. "The Bearded Clams of Madagascar was just a joke. I made a joke earlier this morning. A joke that I never, ever should have made. Because now it has taken on a life of its own, and it's ruining our morning and any chance we have to make any money."

"It's a joke?" asks George, confused.

"The story we are **SUPPOSED** to tell is that we are collecting money to help the children in Africa. That is what we are telling people. Children in Africa."

"What about the Bearded Clams?" wonders George. "Who is going to help them?"

"There are no...they don't need any...never mind. This whole money making scheme isn't working out. Do you want to go to the park, George?"

"I love the park!"

"Then let's go. The liquor store will open in a few hours and I have three dollars."

"And I have 22 cents!"

"Then we are all set. We can get our pint of vodka. After we drink that, maybe I can come up with another plan to raise us up some money."

"Okay, Ralph," says George excitedly. "Let's go, then."

George and Ralph begin to make their way down the sidewalk to the park as a black Cadillac car pulls into Shane and Jim's driveway and three men in dresses jump out. Shane and Jim do not know that they are about to have other visitors. Jim has returned to the kitchen and checking on the progress of the drugs.

"What," hiccups Shane, "was that all about?"

"Just a couple of bums," says Jim, writing off the whole conversation. "It was nothing."

"Did I hear something about," painfully hiccups Shane, "the Bearded Clams of Madagascar?"

There is a loud knock at the front door.

"I told you to GO AWAY!" yells Jim, thinking Ralph and George have returned.

At this moment, Little Anthony, a large bald man with a large nose who is wearing a fuchsia colored Valentino Silk Duchess Satin dress with a jewel neckline, cap sleeves, chiffon flower belt and pleated skirt, kicks in the front door with his white slingback pump. Guido, a slender man with perfect slicked-back black hair and who is sporting a Valentino blue Faberge lace rose silk dress with strapless neckline and mechanical lace roses, follows him into the house. His clay colored open toed Valentino shoes with a four-inch heel strike commandingly on the floor.

Butch and Spike bark, but do not attack. Alvin wags his tail.

"Honey," announces Guido, "we're home!"

Shane and Jim look at each other. Shane hiccups. Suddenly, Jim grabs the black bag of drugs and makes a dash for the back door.

Unfortunately, Big Anthony, a short, thin and wispy bald man with shoulders almost as broad as he is tall and a scar running down the entire left side of his face, is waiting for them. Big Anthony looks stunning in his beige Fango Ruched sweater and matching volume silk skirt. Valentino, of course. It's "of course" because Valentino is the official clothier of the Midland City Mob. The brand is their uniform, as decided by their Godfather. Heaven help whomever is caught wearing a knock-off. The Godfather gets a cut from all Valentino sales, worldwide. If he sees someone in a knock-off, he sees somebody who doesn't respect him. He sees somebody who is taking food off his table. Anybody who takes food off the Godfather's table should expect to pay dearly.

"Goin' somewhere, boys?" inquires Big Anthony, standing on his tippy-toes in his Valentino black patent pumps with matching black bow.

Jim and Shane are in shock. Spike and Butch continue to bark. Alvin continues to wag his tail.

"Spike. Butch," calmly asserts Guido. "Be quiet."

Spike and Butch yelp as if they have just been beaten with a thorny stick and run into the back yard. Spike and Butch were supplied to Shane and Jim by the Mob. They are official Mob Dogs. Trained to kill. Trained to maim. But, otherwise, quite friendly. They don't really like to kill and maim. It's not like they wake up in the morning thinking about it. But it's their job. It cost a lot of money to teach them to do it and they take pride in a job well done. They also know who the boss is. It isn't Shane and Jim. It's Guido. Period.

"Guido," he mumbles, regaining some slight sense of composure. "Little Anthony. Big Anthony."

"Hi," hiccups Shane. "What are you doin' here? You weren't supposed to pick up the stuff," major hiccup, "until tomorrow."

"Just a little social visit," says Guido. "That's all. Can't some friends stop by for a little social visit?"

"Sure," proffers Jim.

Shane hiccups an affirmative.

"So..." inquires Guido, looking around the kitchen area. "How's it going?"

"Fine," assures Jim, gesturing to the meth lab. "We're just cooking away."

"Good. Good," says Guido.

It's evident that Guido knows the situation is not good. When Guido says "good," it is obvious that he means something entirely different. He means "bad."

"Good," says Jim.

"Good," offers Guido.

"Good," hiccups Shane.

"Good," agrees Guido.

"Good," assures Jim.

"Good," says Guido, staring hard at Jim.

"So," Shane hiccups, breaking the 'good' ritual, "why do you guys wear," hiccup, "dresses?"

The room falls deathly silent. You can cut the tension with a dull knife. You could even cut it with a Spork, there's just so much of it and it's just that easy to cut.

Big Anthony and Little Anthony look at Guido.

"Have you ever worn a dress?" finally inquires Guido.

"No," admits Shane. Hiccup.

"You should try it," insists Guido. "It's very...freeing."

"And comfortable," pipes in Little Anthony. "In the crotch area."

"That is what I mean by 'freeing,' Little Anthony. When I say, 'freeing,' I mean comfortable."

Guido is disappointed that Little Anthony has opened his mouth. Little Anthony feels a slight bit of shame. For a moment. Little Anthony is pretty good at recognizing hints, but not very good at following them.

"Dresses are wasted on women," Big Anthony chimes in.

"Women don't have to worry about the 'crotch area' is what I'm talkin' 'bout," informs Little Anthony.

"Men have to worry about the crotch area," says Big Anthony.

"The crotch area," echoes Little Anthony.

"It's all about the comfort," Big Anthony tries to explain. "True happiness is found in comfort."

"Life is short. You should be comfortable," says Guido.

"Comfort is good," agrees Little Anthony. "Especially in the crotch area."

Shane hiccups.

"You got a problem with comfort?" Guido pointedly asks Shane.

"No," Shane hiccups.

"You got a problem with my dress?" Guido says, moving in on Shane's personal space and raising the volume of his voice a few dozen decibels.

"No," Shane hiccups.

"Good," says Guido, turning away.

"Good," says Jim.

"Good," says Guido, again.

"Good," hiccups Shane.

"Good," says Guido, turning back to Shane and Jim.

"Good," says Jim, getting nervous that they are back in the "good" loop.

"Good," finalizes Guido. And he breaks the loop. "So. Enough small talk. Let's get to the point. Are you boys going on a little...trip?"

"A trip?" Jim laughs. "No. What would give you that idea?"

"Oh, well, to be perfectly honest," Guido murmurs, toying with Jim and Shane, "a little bird whispered it in my ear."

Little Anthony is shocked and amazed. "A little bird?!"

"Be quiet, Little Anthony," groans Guido.

"Why would a little bird tell you that?" asks Jim, full well knowing that there is no little bird to speak of.

"I don't know," says Guido, this time moving in on Jim's personal space. "Why would a little bird tell me that? It don't owe me nothin'. Why would it lie to me?"

It is at this time that Little Anthony notices that Alvin is in the room. Alvin is standing, looking up at Guido, wagging his tail. Alvin likes their fancy dresses and well-chosen accessories. He thinks that it makes them look classy.

"Look, Boss!" says Little Anthony. "It's a little dog!"

Guido looks at Alvin and smiles.

"Hello, little dog," says Guido. "Do you know any little birds? Any little, talking, birds? Huh? Do 'ya?"

Alvin furiously wags his tail. Alvin doesn't know any birds, but he appreciates the attention of someone with such perfect hair and good fashion sense. Guido picks up Alvin and puts Alvin's face to his ear. Alvin admires Guido's perfect hair, and it's even more impressive up close. Alvin wags his tail with glee. Jim and Shane smile.

"What's that?" continues Guido. "What's that you're telling me? Jim and Shane are going to take the drugs, sell them in Texas, and fly to Costa Rica?"

Jim and Shane stop smiling.

"Oh no!" says Guido mockingly, noticing the expression on Jim and Shane's faces. "They're going to rip us off?"

The scene freaks out Little Anthony.

"The little dog is talking to you?!?!" spurts out Little Anthony, his 400-pound frame shaken to its core. This breaks the general mood of the room, and Guido is none too pleased.

"Little Anthony?" says Guido, turning to him.

"Yes Boss?" says Little Anthony.

"Please don't open your mouth anymore."

Little Anthony bows his head in shame.

"Thank you," says Guido.

Guido turns back to Jim and Shane, stroking Alvin's back. Guido cocks his head, waiting for an explanation from Jim and Shane.

"We're not...going anywhere," offers Jim, nervously.

"Oh yeah? You, uh, normally have suitcases laying around the kitchen?" Guido wonders.

"That," hiccups Shane, "black one has the meth in it."

Guido smiles. "Oh yeah? Then what's the blue one for?"

There is no answer. Guido looks over and Little Anthony, gives a nod, and Little Anthony takes out a ballpoint pen from the cleavage area of his dress. Little Anthony begins to click the ballpoint pen. Guido begins to circle Jim and Shane, much like a shark moving in on a wounded whale. Alvin wags his tail. He likes the way that the clicking pen sounds. Guido speaks in a very calculated fashion.

"I'm feeling that...my...kindness and...faith...and...and trust in human nature is being taken advantage of. We have a business deal, do we not?"

Jim does not like where the conversation is heading and his voice trembles when he gives his reply. "Sure, Guido, we have a deal."

Guido gestures to Big Anthony. Big Anthony takes out a ballpoint pen from his left shoe and begins to click it. Guido continues to circle.

"I'm struggling with something, boys," says Guido, in a very measured tone. "I want to believe in your...goodness and...and...willingness to complete your business deal with me. I mean, don't get me wrong, it's nothing personal. It's business. It's only business. I mean, I want to be on your side. I want to believe that you are not out to...take advantage of the situation. To take advantage of me. To hurt me. But I feel that you ARE out to hurt me. Financially."

"We would never do that," Shane hiccups, the pain in his chest and throat becoming unbearable.

"Your feelings are baseless," assures Jim. This is not the right answer. Well, it is the right intention for him to lie, but it is the totally incorrect phrasing to direct at a man as angry as Guido is right at this moment.

"Oh, they are? My feelings are 'baseless?' Hmmmmmmm..." says Guido with a tone of voice bordering on complete and utter fury. "You said...baseless? Are you to tell me that my feelings are not valid? That I, in some way, am not valid?"

"No," stammers Jim, backing off. "No way. That is not what I mean. That is not what I mean at all."

"I want to believe you," says Guido without any sincerity whatsoever. Guido looks hard at Jim and Shane. "But I don't. And now Little Anthony and Big Anthony are going to castrate you with ballpoint pens. Hmmm...BALLpoint. For a castration. That's kinda' fitting, isn't it?"

Little Anthony and Big Anthony begin to click their ballpoint pens very, very quickly. The sound of the fast clicking adds nicely to the tension in the room. Alvin loves the clicking sound even more now and wags his tail. He thinks that it is all extremely exciting. It is frantic and feverish. Big Anthony and Little Anthony move in towards Jim and Shane.

Shane is so frightened that he is totally frozen, but Jim is scared into action. Jim kicks over a table full of lit Bunsen burners and the room quickly starts on fire. Guido stands motionless because of his disappointment in Jim and Shane, all the while stroking Alvin's back and neck.

In one continuous move, Jim grabs the black suitcase containing the meth and lunges for the back door. Little Anthony drops his ballpoint pen and begins to grapple with Jim over the bag. Big Anthony grabs Little Anthony. It is a tug-a-war. But Jim's 180 pounds is no match for Little Anthony and Big Anthony. With one, giant pull, Little Anthony is in control of the bag, and he and Big Anthony go falling backward into the wall, knocking a large hole in it.

The flames in the kitchen grow higher and out of control. Shane and Jim run out the kitchen door to the back yard, fleeing for their lives. Big Anthony attempts to give chase, but the wall of flames has grown quickly and he has some of the hair singed off of his arm so Big Anthony is feeling somewhat trepidasious. Big Anthony looks to Guido for guidance.

"Let them go!" yells Guido. "We've got what we came for! Now let's get the hell out of here!"

Shane and Jim jump backyard fences in the neighborhood, running for their lives, as Guido, Little Anthony and Big Anthony bid a hasty retreat out the front door. Jim and Shane scream like little girls. Not typical little girls, mind you. But the stereotypical variety that are commonly featured in "B" movies from the 1970's that contained neither storyline nor acting.

Guido, Little Anthony and Big Anthony remain calm and silent. A house fire is all in a days' work for them. Nothing new about that. Not a big deal. Nothing to see here. Just another day at the office.

Alvin wags his tail.

CHAPTER IV

Guido, Little Anthony, Big Anthony, Alvin and the black suitcase all scramble out the front door of the house safely. They climb into the black Cadillac car that sits in the driveway. Dark, toxic smoke billows from the house and there is a series of small explosions.

Big Anthony sits on top of a pile of telephone books in the driver's seat. There are stilts attached to the gas pedal and brake pedal so that he can drive. He has to drive because he's the only one with a driver's license. Guido's license was revoked decades ago, and Little Anthony has anxiety issues so he was never able to pass his driving test. Guido sits shotgun with Alvin, and Little Anthony crams himself awkwardly into the back seat with the black suitcase. Big Anthony peels out of the driveway in reverse, screeching the tires and literally burning rubber, then drives straight out of the neighborhood as the front of the house becomes engulfed in flames. Which is especially shocking because it's made from brick. Well, not anymore.

"Where are we going, Boss?" asks Big Anthony.

"The parking lot at 12th and Clarkson," says Guido, stroking Alvin. "We are going to meet Scully."

"Scully," repeats Big Anthony. "12th and Clarkson. You got it, Boss."

Big Anthony drives out of the run-down neighborhood and turns onto Main Street. 12th and Clarkson is not too far away.

"You got the goods, Little Anthony?" asks Guido, looking into the back seat.

"Right here, Boss," says Big Antony, opening the black suitcase and looking inside. "Just like they said. 57 pounds of crystal."

"Here," offers Guido. "I'll trade you."

Guido indicates Alvin, and trades Little Anthony Alvin for the black suitcase. Alvin wags his tail. Alvin is quite taken with Little Anthony. Little Anthony's copious amounts of body fat is soft and mushy and warm. Little Anthony is quite taken with Alvin. Alvin can tell by his vibe.

"Hello, talking dog," says Little Anthony. "Hello."

Alvin does not respond, but looks up at Little Anthony with gladness and love and light and wags his tail.

"Hello, talking dog!" yells Little Anthony. "I said, HELLO!"

Big Anthony starts to fidget in his seat.

"Hellllooooooooo!!! Talk, dog! Talk!" shouts Little Anthony. He's getting frustrated.

Big Anthony, on the other hand, is beyond frustrated. He is totally fed up. Big Anthony hates doing jobs with Little Anthony. He has never liked him and he never will.

"Damn it," he snaps, "Little Anthony, the freakin' dog doesn't talk!"

"Yes it does," insists Little Anthony. "He was talking to the Boss! Didn't you see it?"

"No, Little Anthony," says Guido. "I was pretending."

"Pretending?" questions Little Anthony, completely unable to fathom the concept.

"For effect," explains Guido, wildly gesturing with his hands. "It was a theatrical device."

"Huh?" is all Little Anthony can offer.

"He faked it!" bursts Big Anthony. "He fooled you! He LIED!!"

"Ohhhhhh..." says Little Anthony, finally getting it.

"Ohhhhhh..." mimics Big Anthony, obviously hurting Little Anthony's feelings. Little Anthony stifles a sob. Little Anthony doesn't mind being called out for being slow and not understanding things, but he minds having his nose rubbed in his ignorance after the fact. That's bullying.

"Big Anthony, lay off," warns Guido.

"Come on, Boss," says Big Anthony, defending himself. "Why do I have to work with the 'Rainman' here? What's up with that?"

"Calm down, Big Anthony," Guido warns, this time more sternly.

"But-" interrupts Big Anthony.

"Can it," says Guido in a tone of voice that lets Big Anthony know that the topic is closed and the discussion is over.

"Okay," relents Big Anthony. "Geez. Don't get all mad about it."

Big Anthony concentrates on driving, Guido looks through the black suitcase of drugs, and Little Anthony plays with Alvin. Big Anthony stops at a red light as three fire trucks, lights flashing and sirens blaring, go zooming the opposite direction. They're converging on the burning house from everywhere. All over Midland City. But they're not coming fast enough for Doxie.

Doxie, going out into his back yard to check on Alvin, had seen that his neighbor's house was engulfed in flames. He called the fire department, and is currently standing in his yard with a garden hose. A garden hose that is emitting a pathetically minuscule amount of water. Something comparable to a fairly weak stream of urine from a medium sized rabbit. Underwhelming. Very, very underwhelming.

He is wetting down his own house, and the roaming dachshunds in the back yard, in an attempt to keep anything on his property line from catching on fire. If he weren't so freaked out, he'd cry. Mommy, oblivious to the situation, is yelling at the top of her lungs for more Tab.

Doxie is frantic.

Shane and Jim are also frantic, running through backyards and screaming like little girls. They are destroying fences, gardens, topiaries and patio furniture as they run for their lives. And now they hear sirens. Lots. So they run faster and inadvertently destroy more property.

Guido, Little Anthony, Big Anthony and Alvin are not frantic whatsoever. They are quite relaxed. That's how they roll. They are total masters of their universe.

"What's the little dog's name?" wonders Little Anthony aloud.

"Does he have a collar?" asks Guido.

Little Anthony looks. "No."

"Well," offers Guido, "why don't you say some names and see what name he responds to."

Little Anthony holds up Alvin to his face.

"Tony? Vinnie? Frank? Tito?" Little Anthony tries in vein. "Melvin?"

At the sound of Melvin, Alvin barks and wags his tail. Melvin is close enough to Alvin, so Alvin is cool with it. And it is better than "Orville 17." Not to mention the fact that Alvin doesn't have any faith that Little Anthony will ever actually guess "Alvin."

"Melvin?" Little Anthony tries again. Alvin barks and wags his tail again.

"His name is Melvin!" says Little Anthony, fully satisfied and thrilled that he has solved the great mystery.

The light turns green and Big Anthony heads north, towards the intersection of 12th and Clarkson.

"Good job, Sherlock," mumbles Big Anthony with icy sarcasm.

"Oh, Melvin," coos Little Anthony. "I am going to love you and kiss you and hug you and feed you and walk you and sleep with you and pet you and love you and hug you and-"

"Whoa, whoa, whoa, whoa, whoa-" says Guido, holding up his hands. "Hold on there, Little Anthony. We can't keep him."

"Why not?" whines Little Anthony.

"Honestly?" says Guido, not believing that he even has to explain

"Yeah," says Little Anthony, in his best stalwart tone.

The black Cadillac pulls into the parking lot at 12th and Clarkson. Guido stares deeply into Little Anthony's soul.

"Be honest, Boss. Be completely honest. I can take it."

The lot is empty except for a large, white milk truck parked in the middle of it. Big Anthony pulls up four spaces away from the milk truck and parks. Scully sits in the milk truck reading the morning newspaper and eating a chocolate doughnut. He notices the Cadillac, but is immersed in the comics so he does not acknowledge anything other than his amusement in Lucy, once again, pulling the football away from Charlie Brown just as he is about to kick it. Scully smirks and shakes his head.

"Look at your arms, Little Anthony," says Guido.

Little Anthony looks at his arms.

"My arms? Why, they have red spots on them. Red, puffy spots. What's going on, Boss?"

"Well," says Guido in a soothing vocal tone, trying to soften the blow as much as he can, "you're violently allergic to dogs, Little Anthony."

Little Anthony is mortified.

"What?" he screams. "Noooooooooo!!!!"

"You're an idiot, Little Anthony!" blurts Big Anthony. Big Anthony laughs uncontrollably.

Little Anthony starts to hyperventilate, which makes him have a panic attack. Guido gets out of the Cadillac with the black suitcase of drugs. He opens the back door to the car and reaches into the back seat and takes Alvin from Little Anthony. Little Anthony can't breathe. Alvin wags his tail. Big Anthony laughs so hard that tears stream down his face. Big Anthony can't breathe. Guido takes the black bag and Alvin over to the milk truck.

Scully puts down his newspaper and opens the door to the milk truck. Scully is wearing a Valentino silk halter dress with a stunning coral print and a white milk-man's hat. He is smoking a stubby cigar.

"Scully," says Guido.

"Guido," says Scully.

Guido hands the black suitcase to Scully and Scully puts it on the floor of the passenger's side of the milk truck.

"Here," says Guido, handing Alvin to Scully. "Do something with him, will 'ya?"

"Like what?" wonders Scully.

"I don't know," says Guido. "Just don't let him talk. He knows too much."

"What's his name?" asks Scully, laughing.

"Melvin," says Guido over his shoulder, walking away from the milk truck.

Scully looks over to the Cadillac. Little Anthony is flailing around, gasping for air. Big Anthony flails around and gasps for air. Little Anthony pounds on his chest, trying desperately to breathe. Big Anthony passes out.

"Those guys okay?" Scully calls out to Guido.

"You think they've ever been okay?" is all that Guido has to say on the matter as he walks back to the Cadillac. Guido resuscitates Big Anthony so that they can drive Little Anthony to the Emergency Room.

Scully shrugs and puts Alvin on the passenger's seat of the milk truck. Scully starts the engine and pulls out of the parking lot feeing ashamed. Scully knows that whether or not Big Anthony and Little Anthony are okay is none of his business. He knows better than to care.

CHAPTER V

Scully and Alvin drive through town. Alvin looks at Scully and wags his tail.

"So," says Scully, a man who cannot stand the empty sound of silence. "How you doin' there, little guy? My name is Scully. What's yours? Melvin?"

Alvin wags his tail.

"Okay. Melvin," says Scully. "Pleased to meet you."

Scully takes a good, hard look at Alvin. Nearly side-swiping a school bus, Scully returns his attention to the road. He fiddles with his cigar for a few moments. He taps the steering wheel. He adjusts his hat. Scully seems to be thinking in nervous motion with his hands. Suddenly, Scully speaks.

"Melvin is a stupid name. I knew a Melvin once. Third cousin twice removed and I think we shared a great uncle or somethin'. Haven't seen him since I was a kid. Deathly afraid of cats. Total idiot. Couldn't find his own butt with both hands.

Actually, his name was George, but he was such an idiot that we called him Melvin. He was a total Melvin. In case you're missin' my point, Melvin ain't a good name."

Scully disappears for a moment, deep in thought. Again, he fiddles with his cigar, taps the steering wheel, and then adjusts his hat.

Scully looks long and hard at Alvin. Alvin looks long and hard at Scully. Alvin wags his tail. Scully runs a Post Office delivery jeep off the road while he weaves in and out of traffic. Scully doesn't notice. Scully can only focus on one thing at a time. And, right now, it isn't driving.

"I like Oscar better. You're a wiener dog, and I like hot dogs. So here's what we're gonna' do. I'm gonna' call you Oscar. You got that? Oscar? I guess I could call you Meyer, but I knew a Meyer once, too. Another total idiot. A Melvin. Swimmin' with the fishes, Meyer is. And besides, I had an Uncle Oscar. He was a good guy. But they said that he did some stuff. You know. With an ostrich. And a cantaloupe. On a golf course. In Cuba. But they never proved nothing. Well, not in this country. And that's all that really matters in the end, isn't it? So. Oscar it is."

Scully sees a broken down car. It is an old Dodge K-car. Brown with faded purple pin-stripes. The hood is up and the engine is smoking. Trent is standing next to the car, frantically trying to get someone to stop and help him. He has been trying to flag down assistance for nearly two hours. He desperately needs a ride and he doesn't know why his car's engine is still steaming and smoking. It's pretty weird. That nonsense should have stopped a long time ago.

Trent is a middle aged man with blonde hair and a conservative haircut, parted to the left, and he always wears really cheap shoes. He has prominent cheekbones and a wispy moustache. His middle-class shirt matches his middle-class pants. Scully pulls over and rolls the passenger's side window down.

"You okay there, buddy?" asks Scully through his cigar. "You need a ride somewheres or somethin'?"

"Yeah. Oh, man, thanks for stopping. I've been stuck here for almost two hours. I got run off the road and my tire blew and then my radiator blew and the engine caught on fire and won't go out which it seems like it should have ...ummm..." stammers Trent, suddenly taking in Scully's white dress.

Trent saw a story on the news about how the new racket the mob is running is that they pick up hitchhikers and drug them and then the hitchhiker wakes up in a bathtub full of ice with only one kidney. Or no kidneys. Because a lot of people are willing to pay a lot of money for a functioning kidney. Subconsciously, Trent puts his hands over his kidneys.

"I'm...yeah. You know what? I'm...fine. I'm good. It's all good."

"You sure you don't need a ride somewheres?"

"No. Nowheres. Nowheres at all," Trent lies. "I'm fine. I, uh, I've got a, uh, tow truck on the way. I'm good."

Trent wishes that he had a tow truck on the way. He wishes that he could afford a tow truck. He wishes that he could afford to get his car fixed. Trent spends a lot of his time wishing. Wishing and never receiving.

"I though you was wavin' me down."

"What? Me? Huh? Oh. That? No. I'm just, you know, wondering if you have any milk. I could sure go for some milk right now."

"No. All out."

"Darn. Just my luck. Okay, then. Thanks. Sorry to bother you."

"No biggie. Take it easy, buddy. Good luck finding that...milk."

Scully rolls the window back up and pulls off.

Trent watches him drive away. Trent collapses in anguish against the car, immersed in sheer and utter despair. If the mob offered to pay him for a kidney, he'd totally take them up on it. But he can't afford to give one away for nothing.

Scully drives. Scully fiddles with his cigar. Again, he turns his attention to Alvin.

"I'm glad that he didn't take me up on the ride. Funny looking guy, that. Don't know if I could trust him. Shifty eyes. Never trust nobody with shifty eyes, Oscar."

Alvin lays down on the seat and Scully merges onto the highway. "You look tired, little guy. Here. How about you take a little nap. I'm gonna' play you some Ludwig van Beethoven and you can take a little nap."

Scully reaches into the glove compartment of the truck and rummages until he finds the CD that he is looking for. It is Beethoven's Symphony No.9. Scully puts it into the CD player and turns up the volume. Just as the CD begins, Alvin falls asleep. Alvin dreams about butterflies.

CHAPTER VI

Scully's milk truck turns off the highway and into the parking lot of Bruno's Roadhouse Bar. The dirt parking lot is full of newer model Cadillac, BMW and Mercedes brand cars. Every window in every car is tinted, and all of the license plates are personalized. For being in a dirt parking lot that is surrounded by nothing but dirt for miles and miles around in all directions, all of the cars are spotlessly clean.

Bruno's is a simple looking establishment from the outside. It looks tidy and neat. Red brick with a composite shingle roof. And a door. One single door.

There are no windows in the bar. Nor is there any sign of any kind indicating that it is, indeed, "Bruno's." If you are Bruno's clientele, you know where it is. You don't tell anybody about it who doesn't need to know. It is Midland City's best kept secret. A secret hidden in plain sight with one way in and one way out.

Scully parks off to the side of the door. Just as the truck comes to a stop, Alvin wakes up. Scully turns off the music. Alvin looks at Scully and wags his tail. He thoroughly enjoyed his butterfly dream. And the soundtrack. Scully picks up Alvin and the black suitcase and gets out of the milk truck. Scully does not bother to lock the door. Nobody bothers to lock the doors to their cars at Bruno's. Anybody stupid enough to break into anything here would have to have some kind of death wish.

This is where the men in dresses come to meet. It is well known in Midland City that you don't mess with a man in a dress. "Don't ask, don't tell" is the policy here. And, besides, people don't just go by a person's looks in Midland City. A man is judged by his deeds and his actions rather than how he is dressed. Which is how it should be, by gosh by golly. Anyway, in Midland City, everybody knows that messing with a man in a Valentino dress is likely to make you "mysteriously disappear."

In Midland City, a man wearing a dress, or at least a really expensive dress like a 17 thousand dollar Valentino, belongs to a secret organization. Except that the secret is not so much of a secret. Everyone knows that they are the Mob. Midland City's only real gang, organized or otherwise. They call themselves a "Gentleman's Club," but that is just code for "Mob." Everyone sees them every day, but nobody dares to say a word. They just pretend that they don't exist. Everyone who is anyone is a member. Nobody applies for membership. They are told they are joining, and they do. Or else. The mob is all-powerful. They are the all-powerful, never discussed, proverbial giant elephant in the middle of the room of Midland City.

Scully walks through the parking lot towards the front door. As he passes in between two cars, he is careful not to touch them. He is careful not to let any of his cigar ash get on them. He is careful not to even breathe on them. He knows better. They are watching him. And they take no pity.

Upon reaching the front door to Bruno's, the door opens. Scully is immediately welcomed by the familiar smell of expensive cigar smoke and the busy sounds of a very, very popular bar filled with very, very powerful people having a very, very good time.

In huge contrast to the dirt parking lot, Bruno's is amazingly upscale on the inside. The chairs, booths, walls, and even the ceiling are covered with plush, crushed, Italian red velvet. Every lighting fixture is of a gold baroque style, also Italian. Framed portraits of Italy, past and present, adorn the walls. The bar itself is a single 40-foot slab of the highest quality Italian marble that money can buy and smugglers can smuggle. The bar stools were hand-carved in Sicily by master carver Georgio DeStephano when he was 86 years old. A gun was held to his head for every moment of the carving process. The constant reminder that he could die at any second insured that Georgio did his best work.

And he did. The day after the job was done and he was allowed to return home, he hugged his wife, gave her the money he was paid, and dropped dead of a heart attack.

Four antique, hand-carved pool tables sit in the middle of the room. Displayed on them are some of Rome's most famous ruins. The Leaning Tower of Pisa. The Colosseum. The Vatican. And the fourth image is something that nobody recognizes or knows, but everyone pretends to be familiar with. Rumor has it that the image explains the Illuminati. Rumor would be correct. The pool balls are genuine ivory. Made from 12,000-year-old Woolly Mammoth tusk, to be precise.

The carpet is black and inconspicuous. It gets removed and burned once a week for security purposes. The carpet is not Italian, but don't you dare tell that to anybody. And if you did, nobody knows nothin'. Ever. Well, no. Not really. The reality is that everybody knows. The fact is that nobody would dare burn fine, Italian carpet. So they get this stuff from Norway.

This particular late morning, just like every late morning, Bruno's Roadhouse Bar is packed with classy men wearing classy dresses. Valentino dresses. And Valentino shoes. Men stand at the bar and drink expensive liquor. Men shoot pool and smoke expensive cigars. A large man with thick, black, greased back hair and a huge, bushy moustache stands on a small stage smoking a cigar. He is singing Frank Sinatra's *My Way* with the karaoke machine. He is oozing emotion. Grease drips off his hair onto the stage.

But Scully doesn't take in the scene, as he has seen it all before. In fact, he sees it every day. Except Sunday. Bruno's is closed on Sunday. It's cleaning day. It's when they launder the money.

Scully walks over to the most "V.I." of the V.I.P. tables. Moises McSweeney is holding court and surveying his empire. Jeremy and Socco flank either side of him. Jeremy is wearing a purple Plisse dress with a stand collar and cap sleeves. The hem is flounced. It is made out of virgin wool. Socco is wearing a navy colored Plisse dress with a jewel neckline, cut-in shoulders and it has rosettes down the front. Moises wears a stunning, 30-thousand dollar black silk organza gown with floral beaded yoke, stand collar, v-neckline, cap sleeves and empire waist. They drink Manhattans and they smoke cigars.

"Boss. Jeremy. Socco," Scully says with respect and a certain degree of reverence.

"Scully," Jeremy and Socco say in stereo.

"Hello, Scully," says Moises. "How are you, my boy?"

Moises is the boss. He is the boss because he has the most money. The most influence. The most power. The most personality. And the most charm. He also has the most brutality, whether real and true or simply made up and imagined. It is legendary, the stories of what Moises has done to people who crossed him. He fuels his empire with fear. Everyone is scared to death of him.

Moises is a man of God, and his God is money. It is a cruel, unforgiving God. One that causes men and women of all ages, backgrounds and ethnicities to do unspeakable things. Lie. Cheat. Steal. Even kill. Everyone is careful around Moises. And they respect Moises' God.

"Good, boss, good," responds Scully with enthusiasm. "I'm doin' real good. Sorry I'm late."

"Was the morning...successful?" asks Moises, raising an eyebrow.

"Right here, boss," says Scully, putting the black suitcase on the center of the table.

"Good, good," says Moises, smiling. Jeremy and Socco also smile.

Suddenly, Socco's look sours. "What's with the mutt?" he asks.

"You mean Oscar?" offers Scully, putting Alvin down on the table next to the suitcase.

"Oscar?" scoffs Jeremy. "What a wholly unimaginative name for a wiener dog."

Alvin wags his tail and looks at Socco. Alvin likes Socco's dress. But Socco doesn't reciprocate Alvin's complimentary attitude. Socco is also disgusted by the name Oscar.

"He looks more like a...Dean," offers Socco.

"Dean Martin?" says Jeremy, looking across the table at Socco.

"Yeah. Dean Martin," says Socco.

"No he doesn't," Jeremy argues.

"Well," says Socco, beginning to back-track a little bit. "Not 'THE' Dean Martin. Just 'A' Dean Martin. You know. Like a generic one. Drove a bus for 50 years or somethin'. That kind'a Dean Martin."

"Okay," agrees Jeremy. "I'll buy that."

"Well," interrupts Scully, "I'm looking for a home for him."

"Why can't you keep him?" asks Jeremy.

"I have 11 cats," says Scully flatly.

"Oh, that's right," remembers Jeremy. Jeremy went over to Scully's house one time to help him hang a new TV on the wall. The whole house reeked of cat urine and from the second he walked in the door Jeremy had cat hair all over his clothes. There was cat food embedded in the carpet, and it stuck to his shoes. The dry cleaning bill after that visit was outrageous. Jeremy swore that he would never go back. The lure of free pizza and beer just isn't worth it.

"I hate dogs," says Moises flatly. "My mother had a dog. A little one. I think that it was even a wiener dog. Like Dean, here. She loved that stupid dog more than she loved me. I mean, how in the hell is that possible?"

"I hate dogs, too," throws in Socco, always the first to kiss Moises' ass.

"You know," Moises continues, "I think that there's something morally corrupt about loving a dog more than a human being. You know, especially with dogs, I just don't get the attraction."

"This one looks really, really sickly," adds Socco, in yet another attempt to kiss Moises' ass. "And diseased. Why'd you put it on the table, Scully? You wanna' give us all the mange? Is that what 'ya want? For my hair to fall out? Thanks for nothin'. Jerk."

Scully takes a mental note to come up with a list of at least 100 horrible things he can do to Socco to cause him pain and/or sadness for calling him out in front of the boss. As he finishes making the mental note, he is already up to 147 things he can do to Socco. Socco is doomed.

"Maybe you could use him on your show," says Jeremy, also one to always kiss Moises' ass, but usually in a much more productive and helpful fashion than Socco.

Moises scowls. Moises sips his Manhattan. Moises has a vision. Dollar signs appear in Moises' inner eye. Moises raises his left eyebrow. The eyebrow lift is not lost on Jeremy. He knows he has won.

"That's a good idea, Jeremy," agrees Moises.

Socco glares at Jeremy. Scully glares at Socco. Jeremy is feeling really smug on the inside, but he does not let it show on the outside. Alvin wags his tail.

"I could use him on my show," continues Moises.

Moises takes a long sip of his Manhattan. Moises loves thinking about money. Moises loves thinking about his God. Moises spits his long sip of his Manhattan out as he suddenly remembers his show.

"MY SHOW!" yells Moises, slamming his drink down on the table and looking at his watch. "Damn it! I'm late! I need to get to the studio! I'm supposed to tape tomorrow's show in half an hour!"

Jeremy, anticipating Moises' need to leave quickly, jumps out his side of the booth. Socco, anticipating the need a beat too late, jumps out his side of the booth. Socco looks to Moises for approval just in time to see Moises has already made his way out of Jeremy's side of the booth and is already standing. Socco has once again come in second to Jeremy. His soul seethes.

"Damn it!" yells Moises.

Everyone in the bar watches him with uneasiness without ever breaking their stride in any of the conversations that they are having or pool they are playing or drinks they are drinking or meals they are eating. They watch him with every ounce of their collective being without acknowledging that they are watching him. But they are always watching him. They have to. Their lives depend on it. As the Emperor goes, so goes Rome.

Moises runs towards the door, Scully following close behind him with the black suitcase and Alvin. People part and move out of the way as they rush out of the bar. A man wearing a gold, form fitting Valentino dress holds the door for them. He is the man who initially opened the door to let Scully in. He is the gatekeeper.

Moises does not have far to run to get to his car; a black Mercedes Benz. It has a special, reserved spot right out front. The vanity license plate on the car reads "FAITH'A". Little LED lights flash different colors as they go around the license plate holder in a clockwise motion. The chrome wheels on the car sparkle, and the tires are so black that they look like they are wet.

Moises opens the trunk to his Mercedes and Scully throws in the black suitcase.

"Put the dog in there, too," says Moises. "I just got this detailed."

"Aw, come on, boss..." says Scully, always one to look out for animals.

"For the love of-" huffs Moises, not having any time to discuss this. "This car costs more than the gross national product of several third world countries. The trunk is climate controlled. Temperature, humidity, oxygen level, and it's got aromatherapy. I'll probably put it on 'Spring Meadow' for the drive. It's more comfortable than your house, Scully."

Scully smiles and puts Alvin in the trunk. Alvin looks up at Scully and wags his tail. Moises jumps in the car, pushes a button, and the trunk slowly closes on Alvin. Soft mood lighting comes on and it suddenly smells like tropical flowers and fresh linen. The tranquil bliss is shattered when Moises starts the engine and jams it into reverse. Gravel and dust fly as the car backs up. Moises throws it in to drive and peels out of the parking lot and onto the road, headed south, back into town.

The tires smoke on the asphalt and he leaves skid marks as his car feels for traction and gets up to speed.

Alvin sits in the somewhat bizarre calm of the trunk with the black suitcase. Alvin is tired. Alvin is ready to go home.

CHAPTER VII

Doxie has the right of way in the crosswalk. That's not just his opinion. It's a fact, as indicated by the image of a little green stick-figure on the crosswalk signal pole. When the little green stick-figure is illuminated, that means "GO." When the red hand is illuminated, it means "STOP." But none of that matters when you're the rich and powerful. These details are for the peasants to suffer with. Moises's Mercedes comes racing around the corner off of 4th street. Leaping for his life to get out of the way in time, Doxie spills the drink he is carrying. The Mercedes screams down the block and out of sight.

Shane and Jim (and the Mob's) rented house burned to the ground, but Doxie's home was saved by the fire department. Doxie was so thankful that he offered every person at the fire department a free dachshund. They all politely declined. Which was good, as Doxie had no real intention of ever parting with one of his dogs.

They are all his, and nobody can take care of them like he can. At least, that's what he likes to think. He's convinced that nobody is good enough to take care of them. Not even firemen. But Doxie thought that it would be a nice gesture to offer. He was relieved when they all said, "No thanks." So he gave them each a Tab soda, instead. And all his Mommy's cigarettes. It was the least he could do. They dumped out the Tab back at the station, but enjoyed all the cigarettes. Literally all of them. When Doxie wasn't looking, the firemen stole all the cigarettes. They are addicted. They have a very stressful job. It's how they relax.

The drama being over, at least for the moment, Doxie has returned to his daily routine of running errands. He has just been to the dry cleaners and is walking back to his car. He carries four pieces of clothing wrapped neatly in plastic bags. Except the bag on his jacket has been removed because Doxie wanted to make sure that they were able to get the chocolate stain out of the pocket. They said that they did, and Doxie was too embarrassed to check while he was standing there with them, so he waited until he got outside and around the corner.

They did get it out, just like they said.

But now, having nearly been run over, Doxie has spilled his 96 ounce iced tea, sweetened with 96 packets of Splenda, all over his coat. It cost 17 dollars to clean the coat last time. And now it's going to be a rush job and he knows that he will have to pay dearly for it. They don't have any coupons for their one-hour service.

"Dang!" exclaims Doxie, not believing the bad luck. Doxie turns around and walks dejectedly back to the dry cleaners.

Moises' car now turns right onto 5th street hell-bent for leather and then cuts left across four lanes of traffic and one turn lane so he is able to pull directly into the parking lot of the television studio building. In his blind haste, he nearly mows over a young woman walking her daughter in a stroller on the sidewalk. She begins yelling obscenities at Moises, but has to stop when her daughter awakens and begins to cry. Moises pays no notice to this nonsense. He doesn't have the time for mere mortals. He is late. He has bills to pay and possessions to obtain. He is late for an appointment with his God.

Moises jumps out of his car, throwing it in park and turning off the ignition when he already has one foot out the door and on the asphalt. He pops the trunk with the button located on the dashboard, jumps out, throws the keys on the driver's seat, and slams the door. He runs around to the open trunk and looks inside. Moises looks at the black suitcase and smiles. Next to the suitcase, Alvin looks up at Moises and wags his tail. Is he finally home? Or maybe it is time to eat? Or both? No. No such luck on either front. Moises grabs

Alvin with sheer disgust and runs to the Stage Door entrance. The trunk closes automatically.

Moises blows right by the studio's Director of Administration, Lola Bigalow, who does not even acknowledge his existence. She doesn't like him. She can look into someone's eyes and see a person's aura. She looked into Moises's eyes once. All she saw was black fire. She had never seen black fire in anyone's eyes before, and she didn't know exactly what to make of it. But she knew that, whatever it meant, it couldn't be good. Immediately following that incident, Lola's hair fell out and she got diabetes. Now she wears a wig and an insulin pump. She is certain the events are related. And she's frightened. But she knows she can't run. There's nowhere to run to. Once she's seen evil, it's a part of her. Forever. She doesn't fear death. In her own way, she's already dead. Moises can have that effect on people.

Bursting through the doors to the set of the television studio, the usual carefully orchestrated chaos awaits him. Stage hands are making sure the lights are focused and the backdrop is on spike. They are not. The "Moises McSweeney Joy Love Hour" sign is slightly crooked. They work in usual union fashion and it takes nine of them to fix it. Slowly. And surly. But mostly slowly, because being surly requires energy and effort.

The camera men are checking their cameras.

The sound engineers are double-checking the placement of the microphones.

Interns stand nervously in the corners and look confused.

Lyle the floor manager is talking to five people at once.

The two makeup personnel are standing next to the two dressers, like they always do when Moises is late. Which is every single day. But he is the boss and he signs the paychecks every week, so they can't say anything about it.

Lyle spots Moises with the eyes in the back of his head, abruptly ends his conversations, and makes a bee-line over to him.

"Here you are, Moises! We have 60 seconds to start shooting or else we will go into overtime."

"Here," says Moises, handing Alvin off to Lyle. "Put a cone on him."

"A cone?" asks Lyle.

The dressers quickly pull off Moises's dress and shoes. Moises stands, only for a moment, wearing black, revealing, thong underwear. On the front, with real gold thread, is the word "Juicy."

Moises is tan. He spends 35 minutes a day in a tanning bed. It is in his bedroom. The Tan-o-luxe

5000. All the tanning had made his face wrinkly, but he was able to fix that with copious amounts of plastic surgery. Moises is not worried about getting skin cancer. He has far, far, far too much money to get sick.

The dressers begin to dress him with amazing speed into his trademark white suit. Moises likes white. It makes people believe he's pure. But, more importantly, the white color accentuates his tan.

"You know," Moises says to Lyle, gesturing to his neck. "A cone."

"No," insists Lyle. "I don't know."

"One of those...anti-scratch things," Moises says emphatically, losing his patience.

A sound engineer puts a body mic on Moises and he is nearly fully dressed in his clean looking three-piece white suit, white tie, and shiny white shoes.

"A cone," Moises insists again, this time gesturing madly with his arms.

"Oh," says Lyle, finally understanding. "A cone around his neck. Like something for a dog that has just had an operation or is scratching its ears or something."

"Yeah. So he can't lick his balls or whatever." Moises checks himself in a hand-mirror that one of the dressers holds up for him. "Make one out of some cardboard and tape or something. The more pathetic the better."

"Sure thing," says Lyle, rushing off to find some cardboard and tape.

"And then give him to our 'sick and lost' over there," Moises yells.

Moises indicates the sofa on the set where George and Ralph sit. The sofa sits next to a plush, white, reclining chair. George has a set of crutches next to him. Ralph is wearing stereotypical "blind man" glasses and he is holding a cane. George smiles and looks at the lights on the set. George likes the pretty lights.

Ralph is not enjoying any pretty lights. To the contrary. Ralph doesn't feel very good. Ralph is nervous. Ralph re-caps the day in his mind.

They had been going door to door for most of the morning, attempting to collect for their bogus charity, and they were on the way to one of the parks that they sometimes frequent and sometimes don't when a black limousine pulled up next to them. A man, Lyle, asked them if they wanted to be on television. Ralph has never had the urge to be on television, but it had always been a dream for George. Ralph didn't know that it had always been a dream for George until George told Lyle. So that sure was a surprise.

Ralph knows what a dream can do to a man if it goes unfulfilled, especially if you have the opportunity to live the dream and you squander it, so he reluctantly agreed and they got into the limousine and drove down to the TV station. But Ralph also knows what being on television can do to a man, what with all the fame and glamor and all. It can totally change him. It can ruin him. For the rest of his life. And he doesn't want to see that happen to his best friend. That would break Ralph's heart. So he is nervous. But, here Ralph and George sit, waiting to be on television.

Moises admires his trademark white shirt, vest, jacket, tie, pants, socks and shoes in the mirror. He thinks that it makes him look clean. He thinks that it makes him look trustworthy. He thinks that it makes him look like he is good. He thinks that it makes him look like the kind of man that you could trust anything to. Even your very soul. But especially your money.

And he is right. It works. It works great.

Moises receives more than 100,000 dollars a week in donations from all around the world. 100,000 dollars a week in people trusting their souls to him. Tax free dollars, at that.

Right at this moment, Moises is not giving the impression that he is clean, good, nor worthy of the trust of anyone's soul...or money. Right now, he is having a temper tantrum. These never make it on his television program, but they occur every day right before his show.

"Bloody hell, everybody!" Moises screams at the top of his very large and healthy lungs. "Hurry up! This studio time is costing me an arm and a leg! Why am I the ONLY ONE who is ever on TIME around here?!"

Lyle has wrapped some white poster-board around Alvin's head and is taping the end closest to Alvin's shoulders and letting it flair out so that it resembles a cone shape. The poster-board tickles Alvin, and he sneezes with delight. Satisfied with his sneeze-fest, Alvin wags his tail. Lyle is disgusted by the sneezing. He thinks that Alvin must have a cold. Lyle makes a mental note to wash his hands. He doesn't have time right now. Right now, he must get the cameras rolling. Time is money.

Lyle rushes over to the sofa and hands Alvin to George. George beams, and Alvin continues to wag his tail. A loud bell rings, frightening George, Ralph and Alvin.

"Ten seconds!" shouts Lyle. "Clear the set!"

Technicians rush off of the set and Moises pointedly walks center stage. Lyle hands Moises a lemon that has been cut in half. Moises tilts his head back and squirts the lemons in his eyes. First the left eye, then the right.

"Five, four," counts Lyle as the set lights come on the stage and the 'Moises McSweeney Joy Love Hour' sign behind Moises lights up. "Three, two-"

Lyle points to Moises and the red lights on the cameras come on as Moises deftly throws the squeezed lemons offstage. The "I've Got the Joy In My Heart" song plays loudly and Moises begins to sing and pretend to sob with a profound, almost psychotic, joy.

"I've got the joy, joy, joy, joy down in my heart!

Where?!

Down in my heart!

Where?!

Down in my heart!

I've got the joy, joy, joy, joy down in my heart!

Down in my heart to stay!!

And if the Devil doesn't like it He can sit on a tack!"

Moises grabs his bottom.

"Ouch!

Sit on a tack!"

Moises grabs his bottom again.

"Ouch!

Sit on a tack!

And if the Devil doesn't like it he can sit on a tack!"

Moises grabs his bottom a third and final time.

"Ouch!

Sit on a tack to stay!!"

The music picks up in tempo and Moises does a tap dance routine. He can't really tap dance, and the "taps" are really just sound effects, but he totally sells it. This is his favorite part of the whole show. If Moises could just do this part for a living, he would. But, even if it could, it wouldn't make him nearly as rich as he is now. Nothing could possibly make him as rich as he is now. So he considers this just an added bonus.

The music builds to a climax and Moises punctuates the ending by sliding on his knees 27 feet across the stage and suddenly stopping, his face precisely eight inches from the TV camera lens, and yelling "JOY!" Moises always adds "jazz hands" choreography to the end of the number, because it's the only choreography he actually does well, but nobody ever sees it because it is out of the frame of the shot. Moises doesn't care. He'll use that move a lot in his one-man show he plans to open next spring in Las Vegas.

The music fades out, and the camera pans out. Moises pretends to wipe the tears from his eyes as he walks over to his chair. He sobs as the lights come up on the interview area. Alvin wags his tail. Seeing Moises cry makes George feel very sad and Ralph feel very sick.

"Hello friends," Moises weeps to the camera. "Good afternoon! All my friends! I have missed you so much! And GOD misses you, my friends! Where have you been? Have you been close to God? I have! And He misses you! He loves you soooooo much! But there is a pain in His heart!"

Moises inserts a huge, theatrical sob.

"Do you know why? Do you? Do you know why there is a pain in His heart?"

Moises waits for an answer. He looks over to George and Ralph. George shakes his head "no" and Ralph shrugs his shoulders. Alvin wags his tail.

"Because HE needs your love offering!"

"Oh," says George. "Well, I most certainly offer my love."

Moises glares at George briefly, then goes back to his pitch.

"And he needs it right now," continues Moises. "Any amount will help! Do it right now! The address is flashing across your screen! With your help, and with God's help, we can cure the world's suffering! We can end the pain! Please, please, please," highly exaggerated sob, "PLEASE send in that love offering! Twenty, fifty, a hundred dollars...any amount will help! Or, if you wish, you can join our Summit Club. For only a thousand dollars a month, you can sit with me, and you can sit with GOD, on the Summit! We can sit there together, friends! We can sit there and watch the world below us!"

Moises turns to another camera.

"And now, friends, with your help, and with GOD's help, we are going to perform miracles. We have two, I mean THREE friends with us today. Friends who are avid viewers of the program. Please, friends, introduce yourselves."

George and Ralph look at each other. Alvin wags his tail.

"I'm George," offers George. "I'm crippled."

"I'm Ralph," pipes in Ralph. "I'm blind."

Alvin wags his tail.

"And who is the darling, little puppy dog?" asks Moises.

George stares at Moises with a blank look on his face George's jaw suddenly drops, his mouth agape.

"This is, uh," stammers Ralph.

"Uh," stammers George.

"Uh, " stammers Ralph.

"Ummmmmmmm..." stammers George.

"Uh," stammers Ralph, his brain moving at a million miles an hour and fully determined to move on with things so George's opportunity to be on television isn't ruined. "His name is, uh, Lucky. He was in a car wreck and he has, uh, whiplash."

"Oh, Lucky," sobs Moises. "Oh, Lucky, Lucky, Lucky. It looks like your luck has run out, little puppy dog."

"Yeah," offers Ralph.

"But we don't need luck," Moises insists to one camera, then he shakes his head 'No' to the other. "Do you know why that is, friends? Because we have FAITH'A! Yes! Faith'a! Today, my friends, you will be a-healed! A-healed, I say, with the faith-a!!"

"I need a-healing," says George. "I'm a-crippled."

"Yes," shouts Moises. "Yes, you are! And do you know what the path is to healing? Do you know where to start?"

Ralph remembers the answer to this. Lyle pounded it into his brain for the past half hour.

"It starts with joining the Summit Club!" says Ralph with absolute certainty.

"Yes Sir!" shouts Moises, with an even greater certainty. "For a love gift of only a thousand dollars a month, you can be on the road to complete recovery! You will be given the FAITH'A to be a-healed!"

"We joined the Summit Club last month," lies Ralph, his staccato voice exposing the fact that he is having difficulty remembering his lines. "We joined the Summit Club, and we can already feel the power of healing coming over us."

"Yes!" shouts George. Now, this isn't George's line, as George didn't actually have a line here, but he felt that he had to insert something for effect. George is improvising. He was told not to, but he forgot.

"Do you know what I am feeling?" asks Moises, again, glaring at George for going off-script.

"No," says George in earnest.

"I am feeling the power of GOD coursing through my veins!" says Moises, sobbing. Actually Moises is feeling the breakfast burrito that is not sitting well in his stomach, and he is feeling consternation towards Ralph and George for being such lame guests, and he is feeling anger towards Lyle for not finding better homeless talent, and he is feeling an urge to bet ten thousand dollars on "Mildred's Stanley", the number four dog in the seventh race, at the greyhound track this afternoon. So, in all actuality, Moises is feeling a lot of things right now, but none of them is God coursing through his veins. But that doesn't matter. Moises has never made any money by telling the truth. So why should he think that he could start now? He doesn't. So he won't.

"I am feeling the POWER!" Moises yells, continuing the lie. "I am feeling the POWER because of my FAITH'A! George, do you want the POWER!?"

"I want the POWER!" yells George excitedly.

"Feel the POWER!" yells Moises.

"POWER!" screams George.

"The healing POWER!" continues Moises, surfing well over George's energy. "The healing POWER of the FAITH'A!"

Moises goes over to George and, deftly rotating a half turn so that his face is still foremost in the camera shot and George is not upstaging him in any way, lays his hands on George's head.

"Do you have the FAITH'A?" screams Moises.

"I think so," mumbles George.

"You must get the FAITH'A! Feel the faith'a!" bellows Moises.

"I have the FAITH'A!" says George, finally understanding what Moises wants him to say.

"Then feel the POWER!" screams Moises to the camera. "Feel the POWER!"

"I'm feeling it!" cries George excitedly.

"Feel the POWER of FAITH'A!" insists Moises. "Feel the POWER!"

"Power!" yells George.

"Power!" yells Moises.

"Power!" yells George again.

"The power of the FAITH'A!" confirms Moises. "In the name of GOD, I am healing you with the POWER of the FAITH'A!"

"POWER!" screams George at the top of his lungs.

"Then be gone, Devil!!" screams Moises, not to be outdone, again topping George. "Infuse George with the power of the FAITH'A!"

"I can feel it!" cries George excitedly.

Lyle waves his arm in the air, indicating that Moises only has one minute before they will have to take a scheduled commercial break in the program. Moises sees this and speeds it up. He will have to heal them all very quickly. But this does not worry or concern Moises. He is a professional.

"Ralph," begins Moises, but Ralph also saw Lyle signal Moises and has picked up on the fact that they have to move quickly.

"You know what?" asks Ralph.

"What?" says Moises, slightly taken aback.

"I have the POWER of the FAITH'A!"

"How wonderful!" gleams Moises. "Then be gone, Devil! Infuse these two men and this dog with the POWER of the FAITH'A!"

"Power!" bellows George.

"And the curse is lifted!" screams Moises, laying his hands on George. "Cast down your crutches, George! Cast down the Devil's crutches! Walk, George, walk!"

George hands Alvin to Ralph and Moises helps George up. George is still using his crutches. He has forgotten to cast them down. So Moises helps him by violently grabbing the crutches and violently throwing them across the set. They land over by the water cooler.

"I can walk!" shouts George with glee. "I am cured!"

Moises walks over to Ralph and hits him in the forehead. Although Ralph agreed to be on television to help George achieve his dream, he didn't know that the appearance would include being hit in the forehead.

"Well, this is crap," thinks Ralph, "But I've come this far, so what the hell?"

"Be gone!" continues Moises, hitting Ralph in the head again. "Be gone, Devil of blindness! Now take off your glasses Ralph! Take off your glasses!"

Not wanting to get hit in the head yet again, Ralph removes his glasses as quickly as he can and his eyes have difficulty adjusting to the brightness of the stage light. So, for the moment, he actually *is* blind.

"I can see," says Ralph, with as much feigned enthusiasm as he can muster, which isn't a whole lot. "Oh, praise be to the power of the FAITH'A! I can see."

Moises moves his attention to Alvin. Alvin feels the shift of attention going his direction and wags his tail.

"Little dog! Little Lucky! Be lucky again! Your cup runnith over with the POWER of the FAITH'A! Be healed! Have whiplash NO longer! Be GONE whiplash-be GONE!!"

Moises gives Alvin a little bop on the forehead with the palm of his hand. Alvin wags his tail.

"Remove the cone!" instructs Moises. "Remove the cone of pain and shame at ONCE!"

Ralph undoes the tape on the cone and pulls the cone off from around Alvin's neck. Alvin wags his tail.

"He's healed!" Moises shouts to the heavens. "He's healed, friends!" Moises shouts to the cameras. "They are all healed! All of God's creatures, great and small! Healed! In the name of God! It's a miracle! Oh, praise God! Praise GOD!"

Lyle makes a slicing motion across his neck, indicating that Moises is out of time.

"We will be right back after this important commercial message," Moises says in less than a second.

Moises smiles. Moises, Ralph, and George freeze. Alvin wags his tail with genuine enthusiasm.

"And we're out," announces Lyle as a loud bell rings and the stage lights pop off.

Suddenly, the studio is a mad frenzy of action. Technicians run across the stage and the cameras move to their next position on the floor. Some people bark orders and others execute them. It is a flurry of well-choreographed action and is a show in and of itself.

"Thank you, boys," says Moises to Ralph and George. "Good job."

Moises turns to Lyle.

"Get me some hand sanitizer," insists Moises. "I think that this damn dog has ringworm."

Lyle's assistant comes over to Ralph, George and Alvin with a bag of peanut butter and jelly sandwiches and a large plastic bottle of vodka.

"As per our agreement," says Lyle's assistant.

"Thank you," says Ralph, accepting the goods.

"Thank you," says George. Even though, as far as he's concerned, his payment was the opportunity to be on television at all.

"All the best of luck to you," mundanely and unenthusiastically says Lyle's assistant, ushering Ralph and George and Alvin to the alley door.

"Thank you very much," says George.

"Um," says Ralph, "don't you want the dog back?"

"Moises?" yells Lyle's assistant over his shoulder.

"What?" shouts an obviously agitated Moises, washing his hands furiously. "What do you want?"

"Do you want the dog back?" yells Lyle's assistant.

"Oh, HELL no!" says Moises, stopping his furious hand washing for a moment. Moises points at the sofa that George and Ralph and Alvin were just sitting on. "And burn that sofa!"

Right on cue, four burly stage hands lift up the sofa and take it quickly past Ralph and George and out the alley door. Four other burly stage hands, just a quickly, replace the sofa on the set with one that looks exactly like the one that was removed.

"Think of Lucky as our little bonus gift to you," Lyle's assistant tells George and Ralph.

"Thank you!" says George, not being able to believe his incredible fortune. Getting to be on TV and getting paid for it AND getting a new pet. All in one day. And all without having a job or a house or even knowing where his next meal is coming from.

"Do you think that you'll ever need us again for anything?" asks Ralph, trying to find out if he can get anything else out of the gig.

"Ummmm," says Lyle's assistant, ushering Ralph, George and Alvin out the alley door. Ralph, George and Alvin stand in the alley, looking back into the studio. "No. Don't call us, and we won't call you, and, bye-bye."

Lyle's assistant slams the door behind George and Ralph and Alvin. They are back on the street where they came from. They turn away from the stage door and look down the alley. The four stagehands have put the sofa in the middle of the alley and are pouring gasoline on it. They light it on fire and it erupts into brilliant yellow and blue flames.

"Hey!" yells Ralph in protest to the stagehands. "I could have slept on that!"

"Tell it to someone who cares, buddy," says a stagehand with brutal honesty.

The four stagehands use a key to get back in the stage door. They move slowly, since they are paid by the hour. They've done their job. In three hours, they can clock out and go home. Ralph and George walk down the alley. The sofa burns behind them.

"Well," offers George, "that was fun!"

"Uh huh," says Ralph, looking in the bag of peanut butter and jelly sandwiches.

"What are we going to do today, Ralph?" asks George, petting Alvin on the head.

"The same thing that we do every day, George," says Ralph, dryly.

"And what's that, Ralph?" asks George.

"I can't remember right now George," says Ralph. "Ask me after we're drunk."

"Can do, Ralph," says George, satisfied with Ralph's honesty.

"There's that park we like that is right across the street," says Ralph. "The park with the statue of the two people dancing. Since we are already on this side of town, how about we go there?"

"Okay," says George. George likes the statue of the two people dancing. George wishes that he could dance.

Ralph closes up the bag of sandwiches and takes out the large bottle of vodka. Ralph cracks the plastic cover on the plastic lid of the plastic bottle and takes a swig. Ralph and George walk across the street towards the park. Ralph offers the bottle to George and he takes a swig. This is not your sipping kind of vodka. This is gulping vodka. And, soon, Ralph and George will be feeling drunk.

"What are we going to do with the doggie?" asks George, his throat burning with the cheap alcohol.

"I don't know," says Ralph, taking another gulp of the potato-based blindness-maker.

"Can we keep him?" asks George, looking both ways three times before venturing into the street. "Can we keep him, Ralph? It don't look like he eats much."

Ralph crosses the street with George and they head towards one of their favorite shade trees, which has a cement bench underneath it.

"I don't know what we would do with a dog, George," says Ralph. "We're on the move an awful lot."

"The world is a big, bad place, Ralph," says George, stepping over a dead pigeon, "and Lucky here is just a little itty bitty thing. We need to protect him, Ralph. We need to protect him from the big bad world."

"But our lifestyle isn't good for a man, George, let alone a dog. It wouldn't be fair of us to put him through all of that."

George ponders this, but his love for Alvin and his primal urge to protect him doesn't waiver.

"How did you know his name was Lucky?" asks George.

"I didn't," fesses up Ralph. "I don't. But we were having a lucky day, George. We had a job and we were getting paid a bottle of vodka and some peanut butter and jelly sandwiches for it and we got to be on TV. I found out today that it has been a life-long dream of yours to be on TV, George, and we did it. We actually accomplished a dream. That's a big thing, George. Not many people can achieve their life-long dream, buddy, but you did and now we can drink the rest of the day. And most of tomorrow. If we want to. I'd say that was pretty lucky."

"I see your point," agrees George.

"But," says Ralph, getting back to the reality of the situation, "now our luck has run out. Again. It's back to the streets for us. And I don't know that a dog is in our plan right now. You see, right now our plan is to drink this vodka and eat these peanut butter and jelly sandwiches. A dog doesn't really fit into that."

George thinks long and hard about this. Ralph takes a gulp of vodka. Ralph offers the bottle of vodka to George, but George declines. He is thinking too hard to drink right at this moment in time.

"But," offers George, "Lucky sure is awfully cute."

"Sure," says Ralph. "In a sad, pathetic kind of way. Like us."

"Yep. Awful cute," laments George.

Ralph takes another long gulp of vodka.

"Maybe people will give us money to take care of Lucky," wonders George. "I know that I would."

Ralph stops drinking mid-gulp as a light bulb suddenly goes off in his head. Ralph smiles. Ralph looks at Alvin.

"Maybe your name really IS Lucky after all," Ralph tells Alvin.

"Maybe," agrees George.

"I'd bet you a million dollars that it is," says Ralph with all the confidence in the world.

Alvin's ears perk up.

Alvin thinks for a moment.

No.

Alvin wags his tail.

It's Alvin.

CHAPTER VIII

Shane and Jim are in the backyard of 4382 South 18th Avenue. The Higgins residence. It is a nice backyard, certainly better than most they have seen in the past several hours, and here they have found refuge in a tree house.

They have been jumping fences, non-stop, for many, many miles ever since their run-in with the Mob. They have kept off the streets for fear of being spotted and killed. Some of the fences were easy to hurdle, but others were more difficult. There were several city blocks where the fences just came crashing down as they tried to get over them. It looks like a tornado has cut a path through people's backyards. In a way, it has. Shane and Jim feel like a tornado. Fast and reckless and unpredictable. Not thinking. Just doing.

They had a lot of run-ins with dogs during their escape. A lot more people have dogs, especially big dogs, than they ever would have guessed. All of the dogs were quite protective of their property. Shane and Jim have several bite marks on their legs and arms and their clothing is ripped to shreds.

Five minutes ago, they had an incident with an old man who was quite angry that they were running through his back yard. He was happily hoeing his flower garden when an entire section of his fence came crashing down.

"What the hell?" he shouted, raising the hoe high above his head. "Look what you've done to my fence! Get off of my lawn!"

Jim shouted "Sorry," but that was not enough to keep the man from threatening to call the police. Which he did. So now, besides the Mob chasing them, Shane and Jim are part of an active police manhunt. Shane was pretty sure that the old man was bluffing, but the fact that the police are actively canvassing the neighborhood makes Shane think that his assumption was incorrect. Shane and Jim can hear them talk on their radios as they drive by. They are looking for two white males causing significant property damage for an unknown reason. And they will look for them as long as they have to...because they have nothing at else whatsoever going on today. At all. Well, they have this. And it's very exciting for them. Until happy hour. That will be more exciting, so pretty soon they'll all meet there and get drunk and eat nachos and tell stories and lies about their exciting day.

But Shane and Jim were fortunate enough to find an unoccupied tree house, high up in an old, majestic acorn tree. The tree house belongs to Little

Kevin Higgins. Kevin is a bit of a dullard, and is not well-liked among his circle of seven-year-old peers. That will all change in a few years when Kevin turns 16. He will be the first in his grade level to drive. He will be very popular with everyone, because people will have learned how to use him by then. But, for now, he's ostracized and spends all his free time playing by himself in his treehouse. And he goes on awesome vacations because his grandparents are really, really rich. So he's got that going for him. Right now, he's in Tahiti. Feeling just as lonely and unpopular there as he does at home.

The tree house is empty except for a couple of comic books and some three day old snacks in a Styrofoam cooler. Graham crackers and juice boxes. Apple juice, to be precise, made with 15 percent real juice. Shane and Jim devour the snacks ravenously.

"What are we," hiccups Shane, "going to do, Jim? What in the HELL are we going to do?"

"I don't know," says Jim with a mouthful of graham cracker. "Just let me think a minute."

The squirrels that live in the tree look down on Shane and Jim from above. The squirrels that live in the tree know that Shane and Jim should not be there. This is Little Kevin's tree house and those are Little Kevin's graham crackers and juice boxes. This is Little Kevin's refuge. Little Kevin already suffers from unimaginably brutal sadness. Little

Kevin does not deserve this crap. The squirrels take action. They begin to chatter with anger, just like in an old-time animated movie.

The chattering of the squirrels is interrupted by the sound of wings flapping. A lot of wings flapping. It is a flock of pigeons. Two hundred or so. And they all land in the tree above Shane and Jim. A pigeon poops on Shane's shoulder.

"Dang!" exclaims Shane with disgust. Jim laughs. Shane tries to wipe it off with a graham cracker wrapper.

"Okay. Here is what I think," says Jim. "I think that we need to get out of town."

"Well," large hiccup, "DUH!!! But what are we going to do? Should we go somewhere and try to set up shop again? But, I mean, how are we even going to get supplies? We're broke!"

"No," laments Jim. "This is a wake-up call. The problem was that we got greedy. We should have left last night. But we didn't. That is our own fault. And we could have died. We could still die. That's why this is a wake-up call. We have an opportunity. An opportunity for us to go straight. I think that we should take the opportunity. I mean, look at us. We're not drug makers. We're not drug dealers. And we're sure not Mobsters. We don't have what it takes."

Shane agrees with a hiccup. Then, Shane gets hit in the arm with pigeon poop. He tries to wipe it off with his hand, then wipes his hand on his pants. Instead of cleaning himself up, Shane has successfully smeared pigeon poop over much more of his body.

"So what are we going to do?" Shane asks. "Where are we going to go? The Mob doesn't forget," hiccup, "Jim. The Mob never forgets, and I can't go back to jail." Big hiccup. "We could go to jail just for breaking all those fences. I couldn't handle going to jail again."

Jim gets hit in the left temple with pigeon poop. He tries to wipe it off with his sleeve.

"We should wait here until dark," says Jim "They are going to be out looking for us. We wait until dark and we run like hell and we get to the bus station. Have you ever wanted to work on a dude ranch?"

Both Shane and Jim get hit several times with pigeon poop. They wipe it off the best that they can.

"Ummmm..." hiccup, "not really."

"Well, I have a friend who runs a dude ranch. An old high school buddy. It's in the middle of nowhere. Nobody will ever find us there. He'll spring for our bus tickets to get there. I know he will. We can work it off. It'll all be cool. We will become cowboys. We can change our names. I can be Dakota Smith and you can be Montana Jones."

As Shane ponders this, he is hit with several drops of pigeon poop on the leg. Shane stares at it for a moment.

"But," hiccup, "I don't know anything about ranching. Or horses. Or anything like that."

"What's to know?" emphatically states Jim. "You wear cowboy boots and a cowboy hat and you spit a lot. Don't fall off the horse. Don't get gored by the bull. It's pretty basic stuff, Shane." Jim gets hit in the leg and the head by several splatters of pigeon poop. "And riding a horse is easy. You'll get the hang of it."

Shane gets hit in the arms with pigeon poop as he ponders, deep in contemplation. He doesn't even notice so he doesn't try to wipe it off.

"Okay," he hiccups.

"Alright. It's settled then. We will wait here until dark," says Jim.

Shane and Jim can hear the radios from the police cars as they drive by.

Suddenly, pigeon poop comes streaming down on to Shane and Jim like rain drops. But they just take it. They endure it. Because they have to.

They also know that it is going to be a long time until it is dark.

CHAPTER IX

Ralph and George and Alvin sit on the sidewalk outside of Dan's Liquor Mart on the corner of 23rd and Bellaire. Dan's Liquor Mart was once a Mom and Pop organization, formerly called Larry and Flo's and, not surprisingly, was owned and operated by a man named Larry and his wife, Flo. But it is currently owned by Dan who has no wife and had never worked there a day in his life. Dan won the business in a poker game ten years ago.

When Larry met Flo, he had a really bad gambling problem. Flo refused to marry Larry unless he got help for his gambling problem, which he did. And all was well. Larry didn't even think about gambling for 20 years. Until one night when he went over to his friend Jason's house to help him move his hot tub. Jason had two other friends come over to help, too. Friends that Larry didn't know. After the 38 seconds it took to move the hot tub from one side of the back porch to the other, all four men celebrated a job well done with some beers...and a friendly game of poker. Nobody knew about Larry's previous history of having a gambling problem. The only person who did was Larry, and he didn't say anything. That was a big mistake.

Larry was so distraught that he totally screwed up and lost his livelihood on a pair of eights and a pair of sixes that he drank two pints of scotch on the drive home and crashed right through the garage and into the bedroom of his home, killing his wife Flo instantly. Larry got to go to prison for 15 years for drunk driving and manslaughter. Since they had no children or anyone else to contest the loss of the liquor store in an illegal poker game, and even though it was written on a SpongeBob SquarePants napkin, Larry did actually sign the store over to Dan, so the liquor store was gone. Larry didn't care at that point, anyway, since his beloved wife was dead and he was headed to prison. Dan had won the business with a full house, sevens high, and Dan took over as proprietor without any interference.

Dan changed the sign out front of the building, hired an employee, and walked away. After expenses, he earns almost two-thousand dollars a month from the business. Enough to keep him in cans of beans and cartons of cigarettes while his fat, useless ass sits on the sofa in his dingy apartment and watches television. Dan is a very lazy man. Years ago, Dan got too lazy to walk to the bathroom to pee, so he keeps an empty plastic jug next to the sofa for when nature calls.

Dan has not been to the liquor store in ten years. His employee, Brad, brings him cash every month. Dan is happy with the two-thousand dollars he gets. Of course, Dan would not be happy at all if he knew that Brad was skimming off the top and pocketing most of the profits and that he SHOULD be earning 7,500 dollars a month, but Dan doesn't know this. And he is too lazy to find out. Dan aims low, and he always gets slightly less than he wants. And that's exactly what he deserves.

Brad is a smart man. He only sells bottles of hard liquor and blue collar beer and doesn't carry any wine that costs more than three dollars. He sells single cigarettes and lottery tickets in bulk. All of the neon beer signs are donated by distributors, he never uses heat or air conditioning, and Brad has the cheapest prices for miles and miles around. He makes his money in volume. Brad works his ass off, and he pays himself handsomely, but fairly. Brad knows how to run a business, and he's dedicated his life to building up Dan's into what it is today.

Whenever Dan bitches that they are only doing 2000 a month in profit, Brad explains that he only sells the cheap stuff and you're not going to get rich off the cheap stuff. Unless you sell a ton of it, which Brad does and Dan will never know. Dan doesn't bitch very often. He's perfectly happy with a very basic lifestyle, as long as he doesn't have to do anything. He's not greedy. Brad is also not greedy. And neither are Ralph and George.

George holds a sign made from a piece of discarded cardboard and a leaky pen that he found in a trash can at the park. The sign reads "Please help us feed our dog, Lucky." Alvin sits in Ralph's lap as Ralph holds out George's "Cats" baseball cap for donations. Alvin wags his tail. They have been here for nearly two and a half hours.

Several people have donated the loose change in their pockets and purses to Lucky's cause. One older woman, disgusted by Ralph and George's shameless play on people's heartstrings, offered to call the animal control officers on them to take Alvin away to the pound "for his own safety," but Ralph convinced her that they would only put Alvin to sleep since he would never get adopted and, in fact, they were doing him a favor by taking care of him in the first place. Which, in all actuality, is a true statement. He said if she felt so strongly about it, then maybe SHE should just be quiet and adopt Alvin herself. The little old woman gave them two dollars and wished them luck.

So now the grand total in earnings for sitting outside the liquor store with Alvin was a whopping eight dollars and 42 cents. Not bad for two hours' worth of work. And it was eight dollars and 42 cents more than they had made the entire morning from going door to door collecting for an imaginary charity. Ralph and George were pleased, but it was getting late in the afternoon and soon they would have to call it quits. Soon they would need to buy their liquor and go back to one of their favorite parks to claim the rights to their favorite shade tree and bench. If they didn't get there before nightfall, unruly teenagers would claim it as theirs and sit there and smoke marijuana all night long. They learned this lesson the hard way a few months ago, and they won't let it happen again.

The four o'clock bus pulls up in front of the liquor store. Ralph and George have seen this bus before and pay it little heed. George had once wondered where the bus was coming from and where it was going, and at one point wanted to ride it to find out, but Ralph told him that it was none of their business and that George should just let his curiosity die. He told him that wondering things like that would only lead to trouble. But the real reason was because Ralph didn't feel like doing it. But that's not what he said. He made it into a much bigger deal than it was.

And that was the reason that Ralph had agreed to go on the television program with George. Because George, at one point, had some curiosity about something and Ralph told him to kill it. Kill it dead. As soon as he heard it coming out of his mouth, Ralph knew he was wrong to say that. And he felt badly about it. Ralph could have just as easily changed his tune and told George to ride the bus, but he knew that if he wavered at all then George would begin to doubt him. Doubt his plans. Doubt his leadership. Question him. And George would discover that Ralph was wrong. And Ralph couldn't let that happen. He had to be a rock for George, and he knew it. George's mind couldn't handle it any other way. Good decision or bad decision, Ralph needs to make George think that it's all intentional or else George gets worried and upset and starts to cry and Ralph can't handle it when George cries.

The bus comes to a halt, its brakes squealing and hissing and the engine going from a dull roar to a dull idle. The door opens and one single passenger gets off. It is Trent. He is sweaty and his hair is mussed and his tie is askew and he looks much the worse for wear.

Trent steps off of the bus and wipes the sweat and grime from his face. He eyes George, Ralph and Alvin out in front of the liquor store. He eyes the liquor store. Trent wants some beer. He needs some beer. Badly. But he doesn't want to deal with homeless people. He doesn't like homeless people. He knows that he is just one missed paycheck away from becoming a homeless person himself. And he missed that paycheck today. So now he's nervous. He needs to kill his fear with beer. Trent looks again at George, Ralph, and Alvin. And again at the liquor store. He looks a third time at George, Ralph and Alvin. This time, George and Ralph look back at him and make eye contact.

"Busted," thinks Trent.

So in this instant Trent decides to make a break for the front door. He walks as fast as he can and focuses his eyes directly in front of himself. He passes George, Ralph and Alvin, and a wave of relief comes over him. The wave feels wonderful. It's the first time that Trent has felt good all day. And then Ralph ruins it.

"Spare a quarter, buddy?" asks Ralph.

"I...can't," says Trent, turning to acknowledge him. "I'm sorry. I'm tapped out."

"That's okay," says Ralph. "Have a good day, sir."

"And I've had a rotten day," Trent feels compelled to add, not knowing what to do or say because he's never had a beggar tell him it was okay that he couldn't give them any money. And he can't even remember when somebody told him to have a good day. Trent is flustered and confused by Ralph's compassion.

"Bad day, eh? Oh, buddy, you don't know the half of it," says George, not noticing Trent's discomfort. "We've had our share of bad days, believe you me. But not today. Today was a lucky day. Maybe the luckiest day I've ever had in my life."

George thinks about this.

"Well," George continues, "I mean, except for meeting Ralph. That was maybe the luckiest day of my life. But today has to be the second luckiest day of my life. And our dog was a part of it. You need to pet our dog for luck, Mister. He's good luck. Really good luck. He can turn a bad day into a good day. His name is 'Lucky'."

"Oh yeah?" says Trent, totally surprised by the offer.

"Yeah," says Ralph. "I'd say that he was a lucky dog."

"Well," says Trent, "I guess it couldn't hurt."

Reluctantly, Trent leans down and pets Alvin on the head. Alvin wags his tail. Trent smiles at Alvin. George and Ralph smile at Trent. Trent reaches into his pocket and pulls out a quarter.

"No," says, George, "that's okay. You've had a bad day. You just need to go home and have a few drinks and wait to be lucky. Your bad day's gonna' turn around. I know it will. It's gonna' happen."

Trent smiles. Trent puts the quarter into the ball cap.

"Thanks, buddy," says Ralph.

"Sure," says Trent, feeling better about himself now that he has done everything in his personal economic power to help solve the homeless situation in Midland City.

"I mean it," says George. "Your luck will turn around."

"Yeah," says Trent, now feeling absolutely awful that a homeless man is trying to cheer him up. Trent really thought he hit "rock bottom" a few months ago. He was wrong.

Trent turns and walks into the liquor store. The bell on the door rings. Brad looks up from behind the counter where he is reading the daily newspaper. The hum of beer coolers and neon signs drone underneath the static from the AM radio station that is playing old country music on an ancient alarm clock radio that sits in the corner. Brad is reading the financial section of the newspaper. He reads it daily. Thoroughly. Religiously. Multiple times.

Brad has seen Trent before, but does not know his name. Brad has seen a lot of people before, but doesn't know any of their names. He doesn't care to know any of their names. He just wants to pimp the liquor and cigarettes and lottery tickets and let the chips fall where they may to whomever he sells them to. All Brad cares about is making enough money so that someday he can go to Mexico and live for 20 dollars a day on the beach. Brad has a plan, and it doesn't involve getting to know anyone who would shop at the store that he works in and drink and smoke the poison that he sells. And if Brad drank or smoked, which he doesn't, he certainly wouldn't shop at Dan's Liquor Mart. He would go somewhere else. Brad is disgusted by every person who walks in the door. But he likes their money.

Trent goes over to the cooler and picks up a six-pack of bottled beer. The beer is a generic no-name beer. All it says on the label is "BEER." But even though it is the cheapest beer that Brad sells, "at least it is in a bottle," justifies Trent. That almost makes it classy.

Trent walks up to the counter to pay for the beer.

From memory, Brad says "That'll be three dollars and seventeen cents." Brad rarely uses the cash register for sales. He doesn't want to leave a paper trail in case Dan gets up off of his lazy ass to check the receipts. Besides, Brad has been working there long enough so that he knows the price of every item, including sales tax. He knows the combination of any number of items, such as a six-pack and a pint of vodka. Or a liter of scotch and two packs of cigarettes. Or a quart of bourbon, two six-packs of beer, three tallboys, and a carton of cigarettes. Brad knows it all. His mind is like a machine. A machine that embezzles.

Trent fishes around his front pocket and pulls out a five dollar bill and a quarter. Trent forgot that he had a five dollar bill. He thought that he only had three singles. He knew that he had a quarter, however. Two of them. But one he just gave to George, Ralph and Alvin.

"And I'll take one of those two dollar scratch tickets," says Trent.

"This one?" asks Brad, indicating a colorful ticket called "Rainbow Rewards" with a picture of a leprechaun dancing around a pot of gold at the end of a rainbow. The leprechaun looks drunk. And a little high.

"Yes," says Trent. "That one."

Trent's line of sight moves along the row of scratch tickets and he notices another that catches his eye.

"Wait," says Trent quickly, as Brad is about to pull the Rainbow Rewards ticket off of the pile. "What's that one right there? The yellow one."

"It's called Lucky Dog," says Brad. "We just got that one in this morning. I've sold about a hundred of them today, and I don't know of anybody who has won jack shit. A lady won 30 bucks on the Rainbow Rewards, though. Got herself a carton of cigarettes and a shooter of Jack Daniels and still went home with a dollar and 37 cents in her pocket. But the way she reacted, boy howdy, you'd have thought that she just won a new car or a trip to Paris or something."

Trent looks out the window. A police officer is petting Alvin. The police officer puts a dollar in the cap. The police officer tips his cap to George and Ralph and Alvin and walks away. Alvin wags his tail.

"I'll take that one," says Trent. "The Lucky Dog."

Brad tears the scratch ticket from the pile and places it in front of Trent. Trent gives Brad the five dollars and 25 cents, and Brad gives him a nickel and three pennies in change. Neither Brad nor Trent says "Thank you." Those words are never uttered in this store. No courtesies whatsoever.

Trent takes the nickel and begins to scratch the ticket on the counter. A lot of people scratch their tickets on the counter. Shavings of the silver material that is used to cover the numbers litter the counter top. At the end of each day, Brad wipes them into a large mason jar that he keeps behind the counter. Brad usually fills the jar every ten days or so. It is a reminder to himself not to play the lottery. To throw away his hard earned money on games of chance. It is a mason jar filled with the worthless scratchings of people's losses. Technically, it's silver UV ink. But Brad considers it a shining, very real example of their pure, sheer, and utter waste of money.

Trent has six squares to scratch off. He must match three to win the prize. The first one he scratches is for five-thousand dollars.

"This is a bad sign," Trent thinks to himself. It is never good to get the high payoffs first, or 'teasers' as Trent likes to refer to them as. This, Trent believes, is intended by the lottery makers to get your hopes up. To build anticipation. Then they shatter your dreams of winning five squares later.

The second number Trent scratches off is five dollars.

"This is good," thinks Trent. "If I can win five dollars, it will be like getting to play the lottery and get a six-pack of beer for 17 cents. When my wife throws me out of the house tonight, that will make getting drunk on the street very economical."

The third number Trent gets is five-thousand dollars. "Damn," thinks Trent.

The next number is five dollars.

"All right!" exclaims Trent's inner voice.

The fifth number is two dollars. This pisses Trent off. Trent has never had any luck winning on the last number. He puts all of his energy and will into thinking about five dollars really, really hard.

Trent is not sure why he does this, as if he could somehow actually will it to happen, since the sixth number has been printed on the ticket since it was manufactured several months ago. It's not like Trent can somehow go back in time and change it or anything. But Trent tries to picture it anyway. It is part of his lottery routine.

The sixth number is indeed a five...followed immediately thereafter by three zeros. Trent is flabbergasted. His jaw drops.

"I won," murmurs Trent to himself.

"What?" asks Brad. "Did you get your two dollars back?"

"I just won five-thousand dollars," stammers Trent.

"No way," says Brad, wondering if Trent came in to the store already drunk. Brad eyes a baseball bat that he keeps behind the counter, just in case Trent starts to become more delusional or perhaps violent.

Trent runs out the front door of the liquor store and onto the sidewalk where George and Ralph sit with Alvin.

"Hey, buddy," Brad calls after him. "You forgot your beer!"

But Trent pays Brad no heed. He is overwhelmed with the adrenaline rush of winning. Winning big.

"Hi there, Mister," says Ralph.

"How much for your dog?" asks Trent with unabashed excitement.

"What?" says Ralph.

"How much for your dog? How much for Lucky?"

"He's not for sale," says George, clutching Alvin tightly to his chest.

Alvin wags his tail.

"I'll give you 50 bucks," says Trent.

"No," says George, although Trent has obviously piqued Ralph's attention.

"Why do you want Lucky?" asks Ralph, the wheels turning in his head in an attempt to figure out what is going on.

"I'm a dog lover," lies Trent. "And I love this dog."

"He's not for sale," bluffs Ralph, although George doesn't think that he is bluffing at all. George is taking Ralph's word as gospel. Just like he always does.

"I'll give you 100 bucks," says Trent.

"Not good enough," says Ralph.

Ralph's response worries George slightly, as "not good enough" seems to imply that some offer would, indeed, actually be "good enough." That is, if it were the "right" offer, it would be "good enough."

"I'll give you 200 bucks and a case of vodka," says Trent with authority and certainty.

Ralph raises his eyebrows and nods his head 'yes'. George looks at Ralph with surprise. Trent rushes back into the liquor store and heads straight for the ATM machine.

"You forgot your beer," Brad once again tells Trent.

But Trent is in another world at this point. He quickly withdraws his last 200 dollars in cash, paying a three-dollar ATM service charge on top of it. The 200 dollars was earmarked to pay for car insurance, groceries and marriage counseling, but Trent is sure that getting possession of Lucky will more than pay for itself. In fact, it already has. Many times over. Trent is already up 4,800 bucks, minus the case of vodka and the initial price of the ticket.

Trent picks up a case of vodka in plastic bottles and sets it on the counter next to his beer.

Trent slaps a credit card down on the counter. The credit card is only moments away from being maxed out, but Trent does not care. Brad smiles. He is one case of vodka closer to living in Mexico on 20 dollars a day.

It's a win/win situation all the way around.

CHAPTER X

Ralph and George stand in front of the liquor store. Ralph holds a case of vodka. George is in a mild state of shock.

"I wish you wouldn't have done that Ralph," says George, a tear in his eye. "I liked little Lucky."

"We couldn't have given Lucky what he needed, George," Ralph immediately responds with certainty. "Having Lucky wasn't sustainable for the long term. Besides another mouth to feed, he's gonna' need vet care. Medicine. We're always on the move. He's gonna' need a license for every place we go. An' we're gonna' be headin' south soon. I'd be worried about hoppin' the rails with a dog. And don't forget about thieves! No, George. I tell you, it's all for the best. That man said he has a home. A yard. Stability. He is going to give Lucky a good life. Don't worry about Lucky. Just trust me, okay George?"

George thinks for a minute. He doesn't want to let go, but he knows that what Ralph did, he did for Lucky. George feels lucky to have ever met Lucky at all.

"Okay Ralph," says George.

He has always trusted Ralph, and isn't about to stop now. George feels a little bit better.

"Let's go get ourselves a room and a bath. How does that sound? A nice bath, some vodka, and sleeping in a real bed," says Ralph.

"Sounds good to me," says George, cheering up substantially. "I can't remember the last time I had a bath!"

"It's been a couple of months," agrees Ralph.

Ralph and George walk down the street. George whistles a generic tune without a title. Soon, the memory of most of the day will be erased by a tidal wave of alcohol, but George won't ever forget Lucky.

Inside the liquor store, Trent is at the counter with Alvin. Alvin wags his tail. Alvin is happy. Brad wags his finger. Brad is angry.

"Dogs aren't allowed in the store, sir," insists Brad.

"It's just for a second," says Trent.

"Listen, I could get in trouble with the health department for having a dog in here. I don't need their crap."

"I told you, it's just for a second. Nobody needs to know except for you, me and Lucky."

"Only those dogs assisting the disabled are allowed in the store, sir," says Brad, losing his patience.

"I'm disabled," offers Trent.

"How's that?" asks Brad.

"I'm financially disabled," says Trent.

"You and half the country. That doesn't count," says Brad.

"Whatever," says Trent. "I want one Super Powerball ticket. A quick-pick."

"If I sell you the ticket, will you leave? And next time, leave the dog at home?" asks Brad, willing to strike a deal instead of flat-out lose a customer. Every penny counts.

"Sure," says Trent.

Brad begins to push the buttons on the lottery machine, and Trent begins to feverishly rub Alvin's head. Alvin wags his tail with great excitement. Brad pushes one final button and the machine prints out the ticket.

"That's one dollar," says Brad as he thrusts the ticket in front of Trent's face. Trent reaches in his pocket, suddenly realizing that he is not sure if he has a dollar or not. His winning the five-thousand made him forget that he was otherwise broke. But, alas, Trent is able to scrounge up one dollar in change.

"Wow," says Brad, taking a moment to actually look at the ticket. "Your numbers are 1, 2, 3, 4, 5, and 6 with a Super Powerball Pandemonium number of 7. All in a row like that. Out of 73 numbers, this is what you got. The odds of you winning are, like, 500 trillion to none."

"Here," says Trent, slapping the last bit of change on the counter. "Just give me the ticket."

"Good luck," says Brad, not really caring if Trent has good luck or not. He just wants the dog out of the store. Brad hands him the ticket.

"I've got all the luck I need," says Trent, as he puts the lottery ticket in his pocket and picks up his six-pack of beer.

Trent and Alvin leave the liquor store. Trent walks like a man who is on top of the world, his head held high and with a stride of purpose and honor. He holds Alvin with his right arm, and his six-pack of beer with his left arm. The world looks a little brighter to Trent right now. Lines are crisper. Colors are bolder. He has not felt like this in a long, long time.

"How you doin', little Lucky?" Trent asks Alvin. "You made me really happy, boy. I was having one hell of a day. On the way to work, I got run off the road by some jerk in a Mercedes and blew a tire. Then my radiator exploded and the head gasket went out, all at the same time. BOOM. Oil and smoke everywhere. I tried to flag down help, but only one person stopped to try to help me, and it was this strange man driving a milk truck. I didn't like the way that he was looking at me. And he was wearing a white dress. I mean, who wears a white dress before Memorial Day? In broad daylight?!"

Trent laughs at the absurdity of some people's fashion sense.

"I mean, am I a freak magnet or what?" he continues. "Present company excluded, of course," he offers to Alvin. "Anyway I had to walk the rest of the way into work. Then, when I finally got there, I was fired for being late. Right on the spot. Fired by some kid half my age. In front of everybody. It was really humiliating. And this was my third job in two months. My wife told me that if I lost this job that we were through. The marriage was over and done, and I should pack my bags and get out. But then I got this gut feeling, a premonition almost, although I don't believe in that stuff. Well, maybe I do after this. But, anyway, I felt in my gut, like, you know, really deep in my gut that dogs were going to be lucky for me today. So, naturally, I went to the dog track."

Trent remembers his trip to the dog track earlier in the afternoon.

The excitement was palpable. The sun was shining, the dogs were running, and the people were cheering. Trent was cheering along with them. He was cheering his head off. He was jumping up and down and waving his arms with a wild exuberation reserved for times of incredible drama. He was really, really, really, really excited.

"I lost 100 bucks," Trent confesses to Alvin.

Trent again remembers the dog track. Trent stands alone, shoulders slumped, in the middle of the empty bleachers. He looks suicidal and on the verge of tears.

"But then," Trent continues to Alvin, "I take the bus back home, rub your head outside the liquor store, and win 5,000 bucks on a scratch ticket."

Coming back to the present, Trent is quite a different picture.

Trent walks past a gas station and turns down the street towards his house. He stands straight and tall. Proud. There is a bounce in his step that's been missing for a long, long time.

On the other side of the street, Doxie is pushing his car with a modicum of effort. Since his car is so small, and Doxie is so large, the image is mildly comical. But Doxie appreciates that he has such a small car. It is faster to push his car to the gas station than it is to walk to the gas station, fill up a gallon of gas in a gas can and bring it back to the car. It's not only faster, but it's easier. Doxie walks better when he has something to lean on.

Doxie was out running errands when his car ran out of gas. He was buying new strings for his electric guitar. And he got them. He was appalled that they cost 25 dollars. But that means now he only has four dollars in his budget left for gas, and that won't buy him much. And he has a big night ahead of him. Of all the nights in his life that he needs gas in his car, tonight is the one.

Doxie pushes the car up the entrance of the gas station. The station has four pumps, and three of them have yellow plastic bags over them indicating that they are out of order. There is a substantial incline, and Doxie really has to put his back into pushing his rusty Yugo. As Doxie nears the pump, a black Mercedes Benz screeches in to the lot. The license plate reads "FAITH-A." It is Moises. He cuts in front of Doxie, nearly side-swiping him and breaking both of his legs, and pulls up to the pump.

"Hey!" protests Doxie, "I'm next!"

Moises pushes a button and rolls down the window to his car. His bright, white suit stands out in contrast to the black leather interior of the car. It is shocking.

"It's okay," explains Moises. "I am on a mission from God, and I'm in a hurry. I'm sure you understand."

"You're that man from the TV!" exclaims Doxie. "My Mommy watches you every day!"

"I'm God's right hand man," says Moises with his usual disgustingly mammoth amount of pride and certainty. "Now do me, and God, a favor and pump my gas for me. It's not because I don't want to, believe me. It's just that God doesn't like it when I smell like gasoline."

"Yes sir!" says Doxie, reaching for the nozzle. "What grade do you want?"

"God's grade," states Moises flatly. Doxie looks perplexed. "Premium, of course."

Moises has been doing publicity events all over town this afternoon, going from one end of Midland City back to the other end of Midland City and then back to the other end of Midland City. The order of the publicity events that Moises has been involved in was not thought out all that well. It is not efficient. He has been putting a lot of miles on his car. But, this is like most days for Moises.

Busy and hectic and frantic and driving all over Midland City and gaining trust and abusing his star power. He doesn't mind, as long as it all translates into cash. And it does.

He has a big meeting later tonight. At Bruno's Roadhouse Bar. He is going to exchange the methamphetamine for his God. A lot of God, actually. So right now, Moises is feeling especially anxious. He is anticipating that, tonight, he's going to feel especially holy.

He is meeting with a new group of men from out of town. Moises has the opportunity to start up a very large, lucrative new relationship that would bring him to a whole new level of God. And he has the perfect outfit for it. A full length blue silk sequin accented evening KNOCKOUT with a keyhole neckline. A Valentino perfection. He can't wait to try it on.

That isn't the only reason that he is eager to try on his new dress. His pants are bugging the hell out of him. His crotch area has been, and is going to, be confined and chaffed all day. But at least he doesn't have to pump his own gas. A mere mortal will do that for him.

Other mere mortals are performing other mortal tasks. Trent and Alvin have finally walked up to the driveway of his modest, middle-class home. Trent would never put premium gasoline in any of his cars. Too much else that needs to be paid for in his life to be splurging in expensive gasoline. The house could use a fresh coat of paint, the furnace needs to be replaced, and the electrical outlets in the kitchen have been sketchy (at best) since the water pipe burst in the upstairs bathroom and should probably be looked at by a professional.

Even though Trent's home is falling apart on the inside, as far as his job and family, he keeps up outward appearances so the neighbors aren't aware of his struggles. Trent's lawn is perfection, and that makes him the envy of most of his neighbors. The trees are well established, the shrubs are pruned to perfection and all of the flowers are blooming. Trent loves to do yard work. It makes him forget what a living hell the rest of his life is.

"And I KNOW that this Super Powerball ticket is going to pay off," Trent tells Alvin for the hundredth time in five minutes. "The Powerball payoff is up to 283 million bucks. Man, 283 million. I would be a made man, then, that's for sure. It's all coming up roses now, Lucky. You are going to make me rich. Make US rich! I'll buy you a diamond incrusted water bowl, my friend."

Trent opens up the garage door remotely with the keypad on the side of the house. The garage door opens with a sputter and a whir and a groan.

"We only have one problem, Lucky. My wife hates dogs. She had a bad experience with a dog, once."

Alvin wags his tail as Trent remembers a frat house party from 20 years ago...

The time is a much simpler one. Teens were transforming into adults. The stress and pressure of getting into college to get a degree had been replaced by the stress and pressure of actually earning it. But the stress and pressure of real life had yet to kick in, so life was still sort of fun. People are experiencing freedom for the first time in their lives. Young adults think that they really are adults. So they drink and do drugs and have sex. Three things that actual adults who have to lead real lives don't do much of.

It all happened at the Pi Sigma Pi Delta Omega Pi fraternity house on the edge of the campus. Their official motto, embossed on T-shirts and bumper stickers and painted on the wall as you enter the main room of the house, is "Still a virgin? We can help!" The walls are steeped with the vomit and blood from many years of being the hardest partying frat on campus.

Trent is not a member of the Pi Sigma Pi Delta Omega Pi's, but his buddy that he works with at the video rental store is, so Trent got invited to their annual Halloween party. It was advertised as a "ten kegger." One of the biggest parties of the year.

Trent felt good when he walked into the house. He felt his heart leap for joy when he saw "Still a virgin? We can help!" scrawled on the wall with black spray paint. Trent fit both criteria. He was a virgin who needed help to not be a virgin anymore. Lots and lots of help. However, he was unaware that the offer applied to comely young women, and not nerdy young men.

Trent was excited to go to the party, his first-ever social event in his four years of attending college. He was eager to see what the "other side" of campus life was like. Trent lived alone in a basement studio apartment off campus and survived on Raman noodles and MTV. MTV which he stole from the cable box from the apartment above him. Trent was not much of a drinker, but longed to be one of those students who was admired and worshiped as a rebel. As a thorn in the side of the establishment. The degree in janitorial supply management that he was trying to acquire would not give him that, but he thought that if he ran with a rougher, crazier crowd (other than his usual crowd of one, the one being himself), he would attract the type of girl that he had always wanted. One that would get drunk and have sex with him. Because Trent always knew that it would take copious amounts of alcohol for a woman to have sex with him. Trent was a realist.

So Trent was standing in the kitchen, still buzzed from having drank half of a beer earlier that evening, and contemplating whether or not to have a shot of Jägermeister. He had never had Jägermeister before, but knew that it was what the "bad boys" drank and he wanted to fit in. Franny, an extremely attractive brunette with large breasts and a mole above her lip, was on her seventh beer and had just begun to pay attention to Trent only a half an hour before. Trent had seen her flirting with several other men, and thought nothing of it until she started flirting with him. Now Trent felt jealous of the other men. Insecure. Wanting and yearning to protect his new found love from the dirty thoughts and subsequent dirty actions that every other guy in the house wanted to impose upon her.

Franny, unbeknownst to Trent, was only flirting with him on a bet from one of her friends. She was involved in a contest. A contest to sleep with the nerdiest, most insecure man at the party. Franny was in on the bet with five other women. The winner was to get a 20-dollar gift certificate to a local lingerie store. Franny was hell-bent on winning the bet, as she had a hot date the next night with Bobby, the star running back for their highly successful college football team. Franny already decided that she would spend the gift certificate on lacy, crotchless panties. She wanted to have sex with Bobby so badly that it made her ears ring. She knew that he was going to play football professionally, and once she snagged him, she would be financially set for the rest of her life.

What she didn't know was that Bobby already had three children from three different women while he was in high school, and they were already planning to take all of his money. She also didn't know that Bobby had a wicked case of genital herpes and was highly contagious. Franny also didn't know that the five other women she was in on the bet with weren't really in on the bet at all. They were playing a trick on Franny because they didn't like her. There was to be no 20-dollar gift certificate for lacy, crotchless underwear. It was all a cruel ploy to get Franny to have sex with a total loser and then ridicule her about it for the rest of her college career.

Because they were spiteful and jealous of Franny's giant breasts.

They also wanted Bobby's money. They won't get it. However, they will get his herpes. So there is at least some form of payback.

Just as Trent decided to do the shot of Jägermeister to impress Franny, Jacque, the fraternity mascot, came wandering into the kitchen. Jacque was a standard sized French poodle with a seven inch mohawk. The mohawk was held up with wallpaper paste, and the paste gave him a noticeable and annoying rash. He weighed about 65 pounds and lived on a diet of day-after-the-party stale beer and pizza crust and miscellaneous vomit. Some of the vomit was his, most of it was not.

For this particular Halloween, the frat brothers had painted Jacque's mohawk pink. It was painted pink for no other reason than that is the only color paint that they could find in the house and nobody had any money to go out and buy, say, red. Or purple. Or black. So pink it was.

Jacque was an angry dog. He was generally ignored and kept to himself. He had no problem with randomly biting people, and several of the frat brothers were genuinely afraid of him. But he was a good watchdog and he was well known around the campus. That is the one thing that the Pi Sigma Pi Delta Omega Pi fraternity admired above all else. A wicked reputation. Jacque certainly had that.

Trent picked up the shot glass, and Franny smiled at him. Trent raised the glass to his lips, and at that moment Franny drifted off and began to envision the lacy black crotchless panties that she was going to buy after she had sex with Trent and won the bet. Unfortunately, Franny's eyes drifted downward as she slipped into her daydream, and she locked eyes with Jacque.

Now, there were two things that you should never, ever, under any circumstances, do to Jacque. The first thing was to grab him by the testicles. He did not like that at all. So, of course grabbing Jacque's testicles was the initiation for the new pledges into the Fraternity. It was a brutal initiation. The local hospital emergency room was always busy on the night of the Pi Sigma Pi Delta Omega Pi Fraternity initiation night. They always called in extra doctors and sometimes the Red Cross would show up.

The other thing to never, ever do to Jacque was to lock eyes with him. As a general rule, people avoid eye contact with him entirely, as that was the safest thing to do. As Franny soon found out, locking eyes with him was bad. And very possibly fatal.

Jacque leapt from the floor and went for Franny's face. Before she knew what was going on, in an instant, Jacque had bitten off her nose and swallowed it whole. Jacque then ran from the room as quickly as he entered it, and everyone was left in a profound state of shock.

Then came the screaming.

Trent involuntarily spit out the shot of Jägermeister, which landed all over Franny. Every person in the room began to scream and shout and carry on as they took in the image of the completely noseless, very bloody, absolutely terrified and Jägermeister soaked dog attack victim. After a few moments, Franny began screaming and then blood came gushing out from where her nose used to be. Trent looked for a clean towel. Not finding one, he grabbed a dirty jockstrap off the floor and applied it to the hole on Franny's face. The dirty jockstrap later would be identified as the primary cause of a nasty, antibiotic-resistant infection that settled in her eyes. The lingering infection would be very painful and involve copious amounts of oozing green pus. It would have been a lot better for Franny if Trent hadn't done anything. She would have recovered years sooner. Physically, at least.

Nobody knows what happened to Jacque after that. Some say that he went out into the woods to terrorize lost campers and got abducted by aliens. Some say that he went to Las Vegas and overdosed on heroin with Elvis. Some say that, to this day, he wanders the streets of New York City, eating the homeless and pissing on Broadway. Everyone has their own opinion. Everyone had different reasons for finding him. Trent wanted to find him to recover Franny's nose, as he thought that the doctors might be able to sew it back on. Franny wanted to find him so he could get tested for rabies and maybe she would avoid a series of extremely painful shots in the face. The frat brothers wanted to find him because he now had a bigger reputation than any other living thing to ever grace the campus and they just wanted to make sure they could have him stuffed and turned into a bong when he died. But nobody ever did find him. He disappeared forever.

Franny never did get her nose back, and the doctors back then weren't well-versed in plastic surgery, so they just kind of sewed her back up, pulling the skin from around where her nose once was and making a little flap for a single nostril down at the bottom. Franny dropped out of college, her social life ruined, and Trent dropped out with her. She was the first woman that he even almost had sex with, and he was sure she'd be the last, so he was madly in love with her. He would do anything for her. For her and for her deformed single nostril. Franny eventually would have purely unemotional pity-sex with Trent, but only after consuming extreme amounts of alcohol. After accepting the truth that nobody could ever love such a shallow freak as her, Franny consumed even more extreme amounts of alcohol and married Trent. And they had one son. Clarence. Clarence wasn't born drunk. But he was born buzzed.

Franny never got her nose fixed. Since she dropped out of college and neither she nor Trent had ever gotten a job with health insurance benefits good enough to pay for reconstructive surgery, she has resigned herself to living without a nose for the rest of her life. She almost got it fixed once, but the option was either to get her nose fixed or put down a down payment on a house with a nice yard. And, being selfless and having just had a child, she chose the house with the nice yard.

But they never got a dog to go along with the nice yard. And for good reason. No amount of psychotherapy could cure Franny of her huge fear of dogs. They tried. Oh, they tried. And they gave up. The psychoanalytical community had totally given up on her. She is incurable. So a dog is the last thing that Franny and Trent and Clarence ever expected to have in the house. Until now.

"So you see, Lucky," said Trent in a very low, confiding voice, "we must keep you a secret. At least for the time being. Franny is at work right now and she is getting home late tonight because she has a meeting, so we have a couple of hours to figure out how to break the news to her, but for now I'm going to have to put you down in the basement. You will be living with my son, Clarence. But don't call him Clarence. He prefers that you call him Doobie. He's a little 'into' the 1960's. A little too much 'into' the 1960's."

Trent had always wanted to have a child. Especially a boy. He wanted to coach him in pee-wee football. He wanted to take him fishing. He wanted to raise his boy with doing all sorts of boy things that will help him become a man. But, instead, he got a son that is afraid of the rain. He got a child whose first words were, "Meat is murder." He got a boy that would meticulously and obsessively rescue houseflies and "return them to the wild." He got a kid whose favorite, and only, sport was playing Frisbee. Non-competitively, of course, because "competition is wrong." He wanted a son, but he got...Doobie.

Trent stands in the garage next to his unused, spotless work bench and sets down the six pack of beer. Since Trent built the workbench 15 years ago, the only task that it has assisted him in is the temporary placement of beer. And groceries. Sort of like a staging area until he is able to take them into the house. And it has a little radio sitting on one corner of it.

It's sad, really. Trent had much higher aspirations for his work bench than this. Trent was going to use it to help him make furniture for his son's room, repair various household items, and save incredible amounts of money by doing things himself. He was going to save so much money, he figured, that he would be able to buy a new nose for his wife in only five years. Yes, Trent had great dreams for the workbench. It was literally going to be the launching pad for his new and better life. Lots of noble aspirations went into the construction and assembly. But, after his first failed attempt to build a race car bed for Clarence, a race car bed that made Clarence cry because it was so awful, Trent was never motivated to start another project, so he didn't. Now the workbench has just collected dust over the years. When the dust is wiped off, it looks as pristine and perfect as the day that he installed it. Workbenches shouldn't look like that except in sales catalogs.

Trent takes a beer out of the container and opens it with a metal gargoyle head bottle-opener that he has mounted to the garage door wall. The cap falls neatly into a small trash can beneath it.

The bottle opener/trash can idea is Trent's only handyman contribution to his home. It took him a day and a half to complete. It was his "warm up" project for the race car bed. It works most of the time.

Trent takes the Powerball ticket out of his pocket and looks at it. He holds it up in front of Alvin. Alvin squints to make out the form in front of his face. It looks like small piece of newspaper. The same newspaper he survived on for all those years at the puppy mill. And Alvin is hungry. Really hungry. He has not eaten all day. And now he is looking at something that sure looks a lot like food. Alvin wags his tail. Alvin makes a move to eat it.

"Oh! No! No no no no no no no..." says Trent, pulling the lottery ticket away from Alvin's mouth. "This is not for eating. When this little baby pays off," coos Trent, "my wife won't have a thing to complain about any more. And there's no way that she will be able to complain about you. And if she does, I'll just buy her a separate house to live in. And I'll buy Clarence a separate house to live in. And I'll buy ME a separate house to live in. And you can have this one. Or something. Whatever. I guess I haven't thought this all the way through. Doesn't matter. I'll hire somebody to figure it out. But don't you worry, little Lucky. I'll make it work out for everybody!"

Trent shifts the lottery ticket to the hand that he holds Alvin with and picks up his beer. He takes a long, smooth, satisfying drink. With his pinkie and ring finger, he picks up the rest of the six pack and turns to walk towards the door leading into his home. Full of self-satisfaction, Trent fails to notice Doobie's longboard that sits in front of the door. It is painted bright yellow and orange and teal with a rainbow running the length of it, and is covered with modern day reproduced stickers of 1960's rockers past. It has photos and logos of The Beatles, Janis Joplin, The Who, and The Doors. It is hard not to notice the longboard, but Trent manages to do so.

Trent steps on the longboard with his left foot, and both of his feet are immediately thrust forward and taken out from underneath him. Everything for Trent suddenly starts to move in slow motion. He is aware, yet completely powerless. Gravity and momentum are in control, now. Trent is just a passenger on this ride, and there's no getting off until it's over.

Trent drops his open beer. Trent drops the rest of the six pack. Trent heaves Alvin into the air so high that the fur on the crown of his head touches a rafter. Trent clutches the lottery ticket tight, his eyes locked on it with laser-like precision.

Trent lands with great force on his tailbone, causing him to experience blinding pain. But the pain is brief as the back of his head smacks the concrete floor and Trent is instantly knocked unconscious. Blood seeps from the back of his head. The glass beer bottles land next, exploding all around him like little, liquid-filled bombs. Alvin lands squarely on Trent's chest, unharmed.

The violence ends and the room is silent. Except for the blood and the beer seeping down the incline from the garage, it is totally still. Trent still clutches the lottery ticket in his right hand, and he is covered with beer and shards of glass. The stillness is broken when Alvin looks over at the Powerball ticket and wags his tail. Alvin hops off Trent's chest and waddles over to Trent's hand. Alvin eyes the Powerball ticket. It still looks remarkably like a small meal to him. Alvin wags his tail again. Alvin is hungry. Alvin has not eaten all day. Alvin eats the Powerball ticket. Years of practice have allowed Alvin to become very adept at eating, or, rather, inhaling, paper products and other assorted food stuffs very quickly. In only a moment, the Powerball ticket is gone. Now, Alvin wags his tail with great satisfaction.

An old, 1967 WV bus pulls into the driveway. The noise of the bus causes Alvin to look out into the driveway. He wags his tail.

Doobie and his friends Socrates and Moonbeam climb out of the bus after a day of successful recycling. They feel as satisfied about the degree in which they have helped the environment of Mother Earth as Alvin feels about having eaten his first meal of the day. The three hippie youth wander slothfully into the garage to check out the scene.

"Doobie," says Moonbeam in a low-pitched, concerned monotone, "isn't that your Dad?"

"Yeah," says Doobie with a hint of sad knowingness.

"He's been drinking," offers Socrates, pointing out the shattered beer bottles and stating the obvious without knowing the full story behind what is really going on. Socrates does a lot of this. He's very judgmental when it comes to the obvious.

"I know," says Doobie with embarrassment.

"Bummer," says Moonbeam.

Trent continues to bleed.

"Alcohol is just man-made poison," offers Socrates. "Alcohol ruins lives, man."

"I know," says Doobie.

"Look," says Socrates. "Look at the little dog."

"Oh," says Doobie.

"I didn't know that you had a little dog, man," questions Moonbeam, having noticed Alvin when they walked into the garage but also having made a point not to bring it up.

"We don't have a little dog, man," says Doobie. "My Mom hates dogs. She would never allow it."

"Then why's a dog here, man?" asks Socrates.

"I don't know," says Doobie.

"Maybe your Mom changed her mind," offers Moonbeam.

"I don't know," says Doobie.

"Didn't your Mom get her nose bitten off by a Lhasa Apso?" wonders Socrates.

"Poodle," corrects Doobie without any air of correction, but more of a statement of fact.

"So that's what happened to her," says Moonbeam, just as though the pieces of a puzzle were finally falling into place in his head. "I always wondered why she didn't have a nose."

"Why didn't you just ask me?" asks Doobie.

"I don't know," says Moonbeam with complete and utter honesty. "I guess that the topic never came up."

"Fair enough," says Doobie, mollified.

"We should take him down to the basement," insists Socrates, indicating Alvin. "So that he doesn't drink any of this alcohol poison that your Dad so inconsiderately left lying around on the ground."

"Okay," concedes Doobie, shrugging his shoulders.

Moonbeam nods in agreement. Doobie picks up Alvin and they all go into the house. Alvin wags his tail.

CHAPTER XI

The basement door is the first door on the left as you enter from the garage. The garage and the hallway and the basement door and the basement itself are the only interior of Doobie's home that Socrates and Moonbeam have ever seen. And they have been coming over every day for the past 11 years. Doobie, Socrates, Moonbeam and Alvin descend the stairs into the basement.

The walls leading down the stairs are decked out with yellow and blue rope light. On the right side of the wall is a poster of Jim Morrison. On the left side of the wall are three posters of the Grateful Dead. Well, actually, two posters of the Grateful Dead and one poster of Jerry Garcia. The stairs are covered with a thick, beige, shag carpet, as is the basement floor. The stairway is very neat and proper.

Once in the actual basement, however, it is obvious that a teenager lives there. It has a completely open floor plan, as the basement was never finished. Nothing is hidden. Doobie's clothes hang on hangers suspended from a clothesline stretching along one whole side of the house. The furniture is sparse, consisting of a chronically unmade twin-sized bed, a ratty sofa that Doobie found a couple of years ago in the alley, a coffee table fashioned from two wooden apple crates and a chunk of plywood, two end tables made from large wooden cable spools, and an old, beat up console stereo.

The stereo used to belong to Doobie's grandfather. Trent's father. When he passed away, Trent was just going to give it away. And he did. To Doobie. For Christmas. It was all Trent could afford to give him. It is absolutely the most favorite gift that Doobie's ever received.

Boxes litter the room against the walls. They hold old clothes and knickknacks from Doobie's life. There are 11 lava lamps in the basement, but only seven of them are plugged in. And, out of those seven, only five work. The walls of the basement are plastered with posters. On the wall next to his bed are nine black light posters, but you don't really get the full effect because he only has a single 15-watt black light. Doobie has often thought of getting a higher wattage, or perhaps just more 15-watt ones, but has never quite gotten around to it.

Doobie puts Alvin on the sofa and turns on the radio. The old tubes fire up and Janis Joplin's *Piece of My Heart* is playing on the only station that Doobie and his friends listen to. 93.3, KPCE. K-Peace. It is the only radio station in Midland City that plays music from the 1960's. And it's the only station that the console stereo receives. All the other stations are just static.

Full from his meal of Powerball ticket, Alvin collapses and begins to drift off to sleep. Doobie, Moonbeam, and Socrates collapse on the sofa. They put their feet up on the coffee table and nod their heads, knowingly, to the music on the radio.

"Look," says Socrates, although Doobie and Moonbeam are already looking. "The dog is falling asleep."

Doobie and Moonbeam "Mmmmmm..." in acknowledgement.

"I wonder what his name is?" asks Moonbeam.

"I don't know," says Doobie.

"We should name him," insists Socrates.

They all become lost in thought. Very, very lost in thought. Eventually, Moonbeam, Doobie and Socrates come back around to where they started and get back on task.

"How about 'Woodstock'?" finally offers Doobie.

"Heavy," says Moonbeam, nodding his head up and down.

"That's a great name, man," agrees Socrates.

Doobie, Socrates and Moonbeam sit in wonder of the newly named Alvin, and they watch him as he begins to doze off to sleep. *Piece of My Heart* finishes playing on the radio. Jerry Nutter at Night, the KPCE evening D.J., cuts through the silence. Jerry loves to hear himself talk.

"That was Janis Joplin with Big Brother and the Holding Company singing *Piece of My Heart*." It's Jerry Nutter at Night on KPCE radio. That's K-peace, brothers and sisters. Now, I don't know if I ever told this story to you before, but I met Janis in the parking lot of the Winterland Ballroom on April 13th, 1968."

Doobie pets Alvin, who is still on the verge of falling asleep. Socrates fiddles with a purple lava lamp that is sitting on the end table next to him. Moonbeam sits, motionless, his jaw agape. Jerry Nutter tells the Janis Joplin story every day. And Doobie, Socrates and Moonbeam hear the story every day. And every day, it's new. For all of them.

"So, anyway," continues Jerry, "I'm in the parking lot drinking a warm lemonade, because ice hurts my teeth and then I get a headache, and Janis walks up to my van. I was really stoked. I said, 'Hi, Janis. How you doin' man?' And she said 'I'm selling my heart, man. I'm selling my heart.' And I was all, like, 'Heavy.' And she was all, like, 'Do you have any Southern Comfort?' And I said, 'No.' And then she threw up on my shoe. Two years later, and she was dead. I didn't have any Southern Comfort, and then she died. Heavy, man, really heavy." Jerry chokes down a small sob. "I still have the shoe."

"Wow," says Doobie, still focused on Alvin.

"Heavy," agrees Socrates.

"Really heavy," offers Moonbeam.

"And now," Jerry continues, regaining his composure, "Here are the winning Super Powerball numbers for tonight. They are...1, 2, 3, 4, 5 and 6, with a Super Powerball Pandemonium number of 7. Wow. Out of 73 numbers. What are the odds that those would come up? Anyway, I've got a special treat for some of you brothers and sisters. And it doesn't include the Super Powerball, so you actually have a chance of winning. I have, in my possession, four tickets to the "Jimi Hendrix Super Duper Rockin' Experience", TONIGHT, at Rock 'N Ho's. It's an all-ages show, so you don't have to be 21 or older to get your groove on with this one. I'm gonna' give 'em away to the first caller at 555-LOVE. Call......NOW!"

The room is silent. Doobie pets Alvin. Socrates puts down the purple lava lamp and begins fiddling with the yellow one. Moonbeam stares off into space.

"Do you think we should call?" asks Socrates, eventually breaking the silence.

"Huh?" says Doobie, entranced with Alvin.

"I think we should call," says Moonbeam.

Silence.

Doobie pets Alvin, who is enjoying being petted too much to actually fall asleep. Socrates wraps the cord of the yellow lava lamp around his finger. Moonbeam looks at his feet.

After a good long while, Socrates breaks the silence.

"I'm hungry," says Socrates.

"Me too," says Moonbeam.

They sit in silence.

"Waitin' on the first caller for those Hendrix tickets," Jerry says over the airwaves with great excitement.

"That dog is almost asleep, man," says Socrates.

"Woodstock," corrects Doobie.

"Woodstock," says Socrates, remembering. "Woodstock is almost asleep, man."

"First caller!" says Jerry. "555-LOVE! Jimi Hendrix! You don't want to miss it!"

"Where are the chips?" wonders Socrates to nobody in particular.

"Over there," indicates Doobie to the general vicinity of his left.

"I thought that Jimi Hendrix was dead," says Moonbeam, the wheels finally turning in his brain.

"I don't know," says Socrates.

"Yeah," says Doobie, "he's dead."

"Or else he's really old," suggests Moonbeam.

"No," says Doobie with certainty. "He's dead."

"Oh," says Socrates.

"That's 555-LOVE! Jimi Hendrix! First caller!" booms Jerry.

Doobie pets Alvin. Socrates unwraps the cord of the yellow lava lamp from around his finger. Moonbeam looks at the bottom of his left tennis shoe.

"Where are the chips?" asks Socrates.

"Over there," says Doobie, indicating a broad area to his left.

"Do you have anything to drink?" asks Moonbeam, noticing a small bit of gum on the bottom of his left shoe.

"Water," says Doobie.

"Okay," says Moonbeam. "Wait. No. I guess that I'm not thirsty. Never mind."

"555-LOVE! That's 555-5683, brothers and sisters!" Jerry says, on the verge of hysteria. "First caller! Right now!"

"Do you think we should call?" asks Socrates to nobody in particular.

"I don't know," says Doobie.

"No, wait," interrupts Moonbeam. "Water sounds good. I'm totally thirsty."

"Where are the chips?" asks Socrates for the third time.

"Over there," says Doobie, indicating to his left for the third time.

"Where?" asks Socrates, looking around.

"Over there," gestures Doobie. "By the phone."

"Oh," says Socrates.

Socrates looks over and sees the bag of chips sitting on a cardboard box. Socrates puts the yellow lava lamp down and gets up off the sofa with great effort. He trudges slowly over to the bag of chips.

"First caller," offers Jerry. "555-5683."

"Should we call?" asks Socrates, looking down at the bag of chips.

"Sure," says Doobie, making an executive decision. "You're right next to the phone, man."

"Okay," says Socrates, noticing that yes, indeed, the phone is right next to the bag of chips.

Doobie pets Alvin. Moonbeam looks at his other shoe and notices that there is not any gum on the bottom of it. Socrates looks at the bag of chips.

"Why aren't you calling?" asks Doobie.

"What am I doing?" asks Socrates.

"Calling the radio station," says Moonbeam.

"Oh, yeah," says Socrates.

Socrates picks up the telephone receiver and puts it to his ear. Socrates removes the receiver from his ear.

"What's the number?"

"555-5683," says Jerry Nutter at Night, right on cue, as if he were in the room with them. "First caller!"

Socrates dials the number. Doobie pets Alvin. Moonbeam looks down at the floor. Socrates finishes dialing the number. It rings.

"It's ringing!" shouts Socrates with great wonder and dismay. The loud exclamation startles Alvin briefly, but Doobie keeps petting him and he falls back into a general state of complete happiness and total well-being.

The phone rings 32 times. Jerry Nutter at Night finally answers it.

"Hello?" says Jerry Nutter at Night over the radio.

There is a monstrous amount of feedback. It is deafening. The horrible sound travels all the way to the bottom of the ocean. Entire species of sea creatures are wiped out in an instant.

"Hello?" says Socrates, not sure if he should talk into the telephone or talk back at the radio.

There is even more feedback over the radio and on the telephone. It is distracting, and Socrates is really confused by it. Socrates is pretty sure he's used a telephone before, and doesn't remember there being feedback. Or, if there was, it sure didn't hurt like this does.

"Turn your radio down, man," says Jerry.

"Hey," shouts Socrates over the feedback. "I'm on the radio!"

"Cool," says Doobie with great approval.

"Right on!" yells Moonbeam.

"Turn down your radio, man," says Jerry again.

"What?" says Socrates to the telephone while cringing through the feedback.

"Turn down your radio," explains Jerry, "it's feeding back really bad, man."

"Oh," says Socrates. "Moonbeam, turn down the radio, okay man? It's feeding back."

"Huh"" asks Moonbeam loudly, over the feedback.

"TURN THE RADIO DOWN!" shouts Socrates. "IT'S FEEDING BACK!"

"Oh," says Moonbeam, thankful that he wasn't the only one hearing the feedback. He thought for a minute that maybe he had a sudden-onset brain tumor or something. "Okay."

Moonbeam slowly gets up and walks over to the radio. He searches for the volume dial, even though he has turned it up and down and on and off hundreds of times over the years. He finds the knob and turns the volume down.

"Okay, man," Moonbeam says to Socrates with conviction. "I turned it down."

"Okay, man," Socrates says to Jerry, with the same amount of conviction. "It's turned down. Moonbeam got it under control."

"Right on, man!" says Jerry with great animation. "Hey! What's your name?"

"My name is Socrates," says Socrates. "Who's this?"

"It's Jerry Nutter at Night, man!" says Jerry.

"Right on!" says Socrates, enjoying his brush with a celebrity. "We love YOU, man!"

"I love you, too, man!" says Jerry earnestly.

"Right on!" says Socrates.

"Right on!" says Jerry.

"Right on!" echoes Moonbeam.

"Tell him 'Right On' from us, man!" shouts Doobie.

"Doobie and Moonbeam say 'right on,' Jerry!" Socrates bellows enthusiastically into the phone.

"Right on right back at Doobie and Moonbeam!" says Jerry.

"He says 'right on' right back at you," Socrates explains to Doobie and Moonbeam.

"Right on," says Doobie to himself.

Moonbeam nods "right on" in agreement.

"Socrates, my man," says Jerry, "guess what?"

"What?" says Socrates, worried about what he is supposed to be guessing about.

Socrates didn't know that there would be guessing involved. If he did, he would have had somebody else call. He feels unprepared. This has been a huge phobia of his since he was a small child. Socrates prepares to emotionally hide in his 'safe place.' Socrates cringes, both inside and out. He feels alone, afraid and inadequate. He can hear his father laughing his ass off right now. Socrates is about to wet his pants.

"You are the first caller!" says Jerry with profound excitement.

"Is that good?" asks Socrates guardedly.

"Only if you love Jimi Hendrix, man!" says Jerry.

"I love Jimi Hendrix, man!" shouts Socrates, relieved.

"Well, how about this, man. This is an important question that I am about to lay on you," says Jerry.

"Okay," says Socrates, nervous again. "I guess I'm ready, man."

"Do you have three friends?" asks Jerry.

"Sure, man," says Socrates, counting in his head. "I've got Moonbeam and Doobie, and...and..."

"And Woodstock," offers Doobie.

"And Woodstock," says Socrates, finishing his sentence to Jerry.

"Right on," says Jerry with tremendous compassion. "It sounds like you are well loved, man."

"I am, man," says Socrates, having never really thought about it before and getting a little choked up at the thought of how loved and how lucky he actually is. "I really am."

"There are going to be four tickets at the Rock 'N Ho's auditorium waitin' for you, man. Tonight! The concert starts at eight o'clock. Now you and your friends promise to have a great time, man. Okay?"

"I promise," says Socrates. "I promise we'll have a great time!"

"Right on," says Jerry.

"Groovy," says Socrates.

"And now,' says Jerry, "back to some more Janis, on KPCE. K-Peace!!"

Socrates hears *Ball and Chain* begin to play on the handset. Jerry hangs up. Socrates hangs up the phone with excitement.

"What time is it?" asks Socrates.

"I don't know man," says Doobie, having never been one for clocks or time. "5:30? 6? Something like that."

"We should get going," says Socrates with great concern. "The concert starts at eight, but we should get there early in case there's a big line to get in."

"Let's wait a few minutes, man," says Moonbeam, looking over at Alvin who has just fallen asleep. "Little Woodstock is sleeping."

"Oh," says Socrates, finally picking up the bag of chips. "Right on."

Socrates looks in the bag of chips and realizes that it is empty. He is a little bummed. He really wanted to eat some chips. Socrates puts the empty bag back down on the cardboard box.

"Sleep, little Woodstock," says Doobie. "Tonight, we're gonna' tune in, turn on, and drop out."

Nobody bothers to turn the volume on the radio back up.

They sit in silence. For half an hour.

Alvin sleeps. If he dreams, he doesn't remember any of it. He sleeps in a near coma-like state on a full stomach.

CHAPTER XII

It is exactly 7:55pm and the sidewalk is empty in front of Rock 'N Ho's, a mid-sized indoor concert venue that is located in the exact middle of Midland City. The sign on the brightly lit marque reads "Tonight Only : Jimmy Herndicks". The audience turnout has been underwhelming. The box office sports a "Closed" sign, not anticipating any more patrons. The misspelled marquis indicates they weren't expecting many to begin with. It's all coming together pretty much as management expected.

Inside, the rows and rows of red, faux velvet seats sit vacant, except for those filled by the 12 people who have come tonight to see the show. The stage is bare, save a microphone center stage, and a large piece of black fabric covering the raw brick wall far upstage. Down front, there is a green tent in the corner of the auditorium. The large sign on the tent reads "Bummer Tent." It is all dwarfed by the 2,500 seat auditorium.

Doobie, Socrates and Moonbeam stand in front of the stage in the first row. Doobie is holding Alvin. Alvin suddenly wakes up and looks at

Doobie. Doobie and Socrates and Moonbeam look at Alvin. Alvin wags his tail.

"Look," says Socrates. "Woodstock woke up. And just in time for the concert!"

"I can't wait for it to start," says Moonbeam. "We've been standing here for an hour. My legs are asleep. I guess I should have sat down."

"Why didn't you?" asks Socrates.

"I thought that maybe the concert would start early."

"Oh."

"I don't want to miss anything. I'm really looking forward to this."

"Me too," agrees Socrates.

"Groovy," agrees Doobie, finally adding his two cents worth.

Alvin wags his tail.

The lights go down on the audience and two spotlights come up on Rock. He enters from stage left and takes center stage at the microphone. Rock is the owner of the venue. He wears really tight blue jeans and a white T-shirt. He is young, and enjoys being a concert promoter. However, tonight, he is underwhelmed by the audience turnout, but he has had worse. "Special Ed and his Talking Stick" only drew six people over the period of three nights that they played the venue. And the Talking Stick had a really, really bad attitude. He was impossible backstage. Incredibly demanding, verbally abusive and belittling. So at least it's not as bad as that. Still, this evening is not going to help Rock pay for his new jet-ski and chest-hair implants.

Rock got into the concert promotion business with his cousin, Howard, so they could have jet-skis and chest-hair implants. They are shallow people with simple, shallow dreams. Rock still does. Howard does not. One year ago, Howard ate an undercooked hamburger from a fast-food restaurant and his brain melted from e.coli. He doesn't care about jet-skis or chest-hair implants. He just sits in his wheelchair at the assisted living home and drools. Howard is lucky to be alive, but he doesn't remember his own name. His care is expensive. His lawsuit against the fast food restaurant is tied up in court and probably will be for years and years to come. For now, there will be no jet-skis and chest-hair implants. They will happen, though. Rock is determined.

"Hey, everybody!" booms Rock into the microphone, his voice large and echoing through the cavernous room. "Thanks for coming to Rock 'N Ho's! Are you ready to rock!?"

There is no response from the audience. Doobie, Socrates and Moonbeam smile. Alvin wags his tail.

"I said," yells Rock, "are you ready to ROCK!?"

There is still no response.

"Okay," concedes Rock. "Well, I want to welcome you all to Rock 'N Ho's. Tonight, we are privileged to present to you, The Jimi Hendrix Super Duper Rockin' Experience!"

Socrates and Moonbeam clap. Doobie nods his head up and down.

Alvin wags his tail.

"Right on," says Rock, as he watches Socrates and Moonbeam clap. "But first, I have one announcement."

Rock pulls a scrap of paper from his pocket.

"Don't take the yellow acid," Rock reads. "The yellow acid is BAD."

Suddenly, an elderly hippie wearing a "Remember Kent State" T-shirt, cut off blue jean shorts and brown hemp sandals, stands up on his seat and takes notice. He is in the fifth row, off to the side.

"What did you say?" asks the elderly hippie.

"The yellow acid...is BAD!" shouts Rock.

"Oh NO!" yells the elderly hippie.

"I repeat," says Rock, "the yellow acid is BAD. Whatever you do tonight, DON'T take the yellow acid!"

"Son of a BITCH!" screams the elderly hippie, "I just took three hits! What am I gonna' do?"

"Stay calm and go to the Bummer Tent," says Rock calmly. Although, with his voice amplified to the point of near distortion, Rock sounds loud and frightening. Which sounds even worse if you are under the influence of three hits of really bad LSD.

"Go straight to the Bummer Tent, dude," Rock reiterates.

"Where?" screams the elderly hippie.

"Right over there, man," says Rock, pointing to the corner of the stage.

"What?" cries the elderly hippie.

"The Bummer Tent. Right there," says Rock. "The tent."

"Huh?" queries the elderly hippie.

"There," says Rock. "The tent. The tent that says 'Bummer Tent' on it. It's green. The only tent in here. Right over there."

"Oh, man," laments the elderly hippie as he trudges begrudgingly towards the tent, "I don't need this crap!"

The elderly hippie arrives at the bummer tent and starts crying. A doctor and two nurses attend to him.

"Alright," shouts Rock, trying to get the show started because, as everybody knows, the sooner you start the sooner you finish. And the sooner you finish, the sooner you get to go home. And the sooner you go home, the sooner you can look at pornography downloaded for free off the internet on a 75 inch, 3-D television. "Now, I present to you, the one...the only...Jimi Hendrix! No refunds."

Rock quickly exits the stage to a mere smattering of applause. Rock enthusiastically smiles and waves to the audience out of habit as he leaves. If he were paying attention, he'd notice that he's smiling and waving at empty chairs.

Doxie takes the stage decked out in a broadly striped orange, purple, yellow and green suit with a psychedelically patterned silk jacket. He wears a bright pink feathered boa and a "Westerner" style hat crowned with a star-like broach, a set of silver bangles, and an angled feather. Doxie has a brown and purple silk scarf tied to his right arm, and a green and red silk scarf tied to his right leg. Doxie's white shirt does not quite cover all of his belly, and his pants don't quite cover his butt-crack.

Doxie carries an electric guitar. Doxie walks up to the microphone with a swagger.

"Good evening, my brothers and sisters!" shouts Doxie into the microphone. The auditorium is silent. "Let's rock!"

Alvin loves to "rock". At least, he thinks that he does. He has never done it before. Alvin wags his tail with anticipation. He is excited to try it out.

The lights go down further on the audience so that all you can see are the "EXIT" signs. A purple light illuminates the stage. Doxie double-checks his fingering on his axe. Doxie nods to an unseen person stage right, and a CD of "Purple Haze", minus the vocals and lead guitar part, blasts through the auditorium. Doxie plays his guitar, and he is incredible.

Doxie balances precariously on his right foot and maneuvers the guitar so that he can play it under his left leg. This is quite a stretch for him, literally and figuratively. He has torn muscles in both his back, legs and right arm while attempting this feat. But he pulls it off. In fact, he makes it look easy. Doxie changes positions and plays the guitar behind his head.

Doxie brings the guitar up to his mouth and plays the guitar with his teeth. Doxie's shirt does not quite cover all of his belly, and his pants don't quite cover his butt-crack. Doobie smiles. Socrates and Moonbeam clap.

"Groovy!" yells Socrates.

"Right on!" yells Moonbeam.

"Heavy!" yells Doobie.

Alvin wags his tail. Alvin has decided that he absolutely LOVES to "rock out."

The song is almost over, and it is time for Doxie to pull out all the stops. He attempts to pull off his greatest stunt for the finale: playing the guitar behind his back. This is the maneuver that left him bed-ridden for three days and nearly got Alvin euthanized at the dog shelter. Doxie holds the neck of the guitar with his left hand and arches his spine. He gets the guitar wedged in to the small of his back and is able to strum out four chords before aborting the feat.

Doxie is fully satisfied with his performance. He lays the guitar on the stage, reaches into his pocket for a container of lighter fluid and a lighter, and douses the guitar with the fluid. Doxie lights his guitar on fire and beckons the flames to grow higher.

They obey, and they do.

Socrates and Moonbeam clap. Doobie smiles. Alvin wags his tail.

A heavily tattooed stagehand runs out onto the stage. He is wearing combat boots and an "Anarchy" T-shirt. He has a mohawk haircut and his eyebrows are pierced. He carries a large fire department approved Class ABC dry chemical fire extinguisher, and he puts out the fire very quickly. The powder from the extinguisher floats over the stage and into the front row and the residue settles gently on Doobie, Socrates, Moonbeam, and Alvin. They are so enthralled with the show that they don't even notice.

The stagehand runs off the stage and Doxie picks up the guitar, lifting it high over his head. In one, giant, over-exaggerated motion, Doxie smashes the guitar onto the stage and it shatters into a million pieces.

The song on the CD ends.

The guitar is smashed.

Silence.

The song is over.

The set is over.

The evening is over, two minutes and forty-six seconds after it began. "The Jimi Hendrix Super Duper Rockin' Experience" has come to an end.

The auditorium is silent. Somewhere, someone coughs.

"I thought that song had words," says Socrates.

"What?" asks Moonbeam.

"I thought that song had, you know, lyrics. Words. Singing," says Socrates.

"Oh!" says Moonbeam, understanding that considering.

"Words!" says Doobie, also understanding and considering.

"Yeah," says Socrates.

"I don't know," says Moonbeam.

"Let's go ask him," says Doobie.

"Okay," says Socrates.

Moonbeam shrugs his shoulders.

Alvin wags his tail.

Somewhere, someone else coughs.

"Thank you," shouts Doxie into the microphone, "thank you and good night! Drive safe!"

Doxie flashes a peace sign with his fingers and exits the stage in silence. The lights go down to black on the stage and come up to full in the audience.

"Groovy!" says Socrates.

"Right on!" says Moonbeam.

"Heavy!" says Doobie.

Alvin wags his tail.

The audience begins to file out of the auditorium in an orderly fashion. Doobie, Alvin, Socrates and Moonbeam follow them. The elderly hippie man begins to freak out in the Bummer Tent. He is frothing at the mouth and is tightly bound with a straight jacket.

"Worms are eating my brain!" he shouts to the doctor and two nurses. "Bats! Watch out for the bats! There are bats everywhere!"

The doctor and two nurses just nod at each other, knowingly.

"Kill me," cries the elderly hippie. "Just kill me!"

The doctor and two nurses continue to nod. They know that they won't have to kill him. Father Time will do that soon enough. And, besides, in about 20 minutes, he'll never remember his own

name again. That is what bad acid, and e. coli from
a bad hamburger, will do to you.

CHAPTER XIII

Doobie, Alvin, Socrates and Moonbeam stand patiently outside the stage door in the alley of Rock 'N Ho's. They went straight there as soon as they left the auditorium. They are still blanketed in Class ABC dry powder fire extinguisher residue. Their eyes are burning, but their flesh is protected from fires involving most solids, liquids and gasses. However, they are still vulnerable to fire involving metals and electrical apparatus. Socrates knows this, and it makes him a little more nervous than usual. He's trying to deal with it the best he can.

Doobie holds Alvin. Everyone's ears are ringing. Even Alvin's.

"This must be one of the side effects of 'rocking out'," thinks Alvin, barely able to hear his voice inside his head. But he doesn't care. It is a price worth paying. Alvin wags his tail.

Finally, Doxie comes out of the stage door, still in full Jimi Hendrix regalia. Doxie is sweating profusely, every pore of his body squeezing out as much donut and hamburger infused body juice it possibly can. His body wants to get clean. It really does. But Doxie doesn't. Personal health is an afterthought to Doxie. It's all about the art. A thoroughly sweat-soaked towel drapes over his neck like a cape.

"That was awesome," gushes Socrates.

"Thanks, kid," says Doxie. "I got a cramp in my leg right there at the end, but I sucked it up and I powered through it. I didn't have a choice."

"You are amazing," says Doobie.

"Yeah, I know," agrees Doxie. "Here is a souvenir."

Doxie throws his dripping wet towel to Doobie. It hits Doobie and Alvin in the face and falls to the ground. Half of Doobie's face and half of Alvin is drenched with Doxie's sweat. It smells like meatballs. Doobie bends down and picks the towel up.

"Thanks!" exclaims Doobie gratefully.

"Sure," says Doxie. "No problem, kid."

"Are there words to that song?" asks Socrates.

"Huh?" asks Doxie.

"Words," says Moonbeam.

"Lyrics," says Doobie.

"For the song in your concert," says Socrates.

"Yeah," concedes Doxie. "There are words. I forgot to sing. Was it obvious?"

"Not really," says Socrates.

"No," says Moonbeam.

"I didn't notice at all," says Doobie. "You're so awesome!"

Doxie is enjoying the compliments, but he suddenly keys in on Alvin, his eyes locked on him with total focus. He didn't really know Alvin was a dog at first. He just sort of blended in with the powdered donut-like teenagers. But now Doxie's sure of it. It's a dog. It could even be a dachshund. He is now suddenly obsessed with Alvin. Doxie drools.

"Cool dog, man," Doxie tells Doobie, a frothy slaver oozing from the corners of his mouth.

"Thanks," says Doobie.

"Will you sign my forehead?" asks Socrates, breaking Doxie's concentrated preoccupation with Alvin.

"You got a pen?" asks Doxie.

Socrates searches his pockets for a pen. Doxie stares at Alvin. Moonbeam searches his pockets for a moment, very quickly losing interest in looking and fully content in standing and doing nothing at all. Socrates checks his pockets over and over again. Doxie looks at Alvin so hard he can feel his brainwaves. Socrates checks his shoes for a pen. Socrates checks his pockets one more time, but still can't find one.

"Oh, wait," says Doxie, suddenly and very matter-of-factly. "I've got one."

Doxie pulls out a fat, black permanent marker from inside his breast pocket. Doxie pulls off the cap, smells the marker with an almost perverse joy, and then scrawls "Jimi Hendrix" on Socrates' forehead. The letters are illegible. Doxie writes like a drunken three-year-old child.

"You are awesome!" gushes Socrates.

Doxie ignores the compliment and is once again totally obsessed with Alvin and how to get him.

"That's a really groovy looking dog, man," Doxie tells Doobie.

"His name is Woodstock," offers Doobie.

"Woodstock," says Doxie, taking it in. "That's groovy. I can dig it, man."

"He's a stray," continues Doobie. "He doesn't have a collar or anything. I think that my dad brought him home."

"You don't know for sure?" questions Doxie.

"Doobie's dad's a drunk-aholic," offers Socrates.

"Oh, I'm sorry to hear that," says Doxie. "My Dad liked prescription pills and peanut butter and banana sandwiches."

"Right on," say Doobie, Socrates and Moonbeam in perfect unison.

"But you think he's a stray, huh?" says Doxie, the adrenaline beginning to percolate from the depths of his very being. "That's wicked."

"Yeah," says Doobie.

"Is that, a, uh, a dachshund?" asks Doxie, almost too quickly.

"Yeah," says Moonbeam. "I guess so. Either that, or it's a wiener dog."

"Is it a male or a female?" asks Doxie, definitely too quickly.

"I think it's a him," guesses Doobie. "I think."

"Oh yeah?" says Doxie. "What makes you think that?"

"Well," offers Doobie, "he's got a penis and stuff."

"I agree," says Socrates, not wanting to be left out.

"All right. I'm hearin' ya', man. Heavy," says Doxie.

"I don't know too much about dogs," confesses Doobie. "I've never had a dog."

"Oh, no?" questions Doxie, unable to comprehend such a travesty.

"No," replies Doobie. "My mom got her nose bitten off by a poodle when she was in college."

"Oh," retorts Doxie, somewhat stunned. "But, anyway, yeah, a penis is how you tell if it's a boy or not."

Doxie is about to drop dead from dog envy.

"Well, I wasn't sure," says Doobie. "In case he was neutered or something. Or, whatever."

"No," gently corrects Doxie, "if he were neutered he'd still have a penis."

"Heavy," says Socrates.

"I don't know if I can keep him or not, but he's a great little dog," laments Doobie.

"A little *boy* dog," confirms Moonbeam.

"You can't keep him?" blurts out Doxie, his eyes growing large and eyebrows standing on end.

"Maybe you could take him," offers Doobie.

Doxie stares blankly at Doobie as he melts inside. But his total lack of emotion worries Doobie, Moonbeam and Socrates.

"He's really easy going," says Socrates.

"And he loved your show," adds Moonbeam.

"Well..." says Doxie, coming out of his happy-coma. "I guess I could maybe give him a home."

"Yeah?" says Doobie.

"Yeah," says Doxie. "I already have a couple of dogs. Dachshunds, coincidentally. He'd fit right in."

"Right on!" says Doobie.

"Right on!" says Socrates.

"Right on!" says Moonbeam.

"Right on!" says Doxie, capping the "right on"-ness of the moment.

"Here, little fella." Doxie says as he snatches Alvin from Doobie. "I think I'll call you...Peabody 18."

"But his name is Woodstock," corrects Doobie.

"I've already got a dog named Woodstock," lies Doxie. "It would be too confusing to have two dogs with the same name. Well, not confusing for me, but for the dogs. They wouldn't know which one I was referring to."

"Oh," murmurs Doobie, contemplating the confusion.

"Peabody 18. Heavy," states Socrates.

"Heavy duty," agrees Doxie.

"Well, I gotta' go. I have a radio interview that I need to get to."

"Really?" gushes Moonbeam. "Cool."

"Yeah," Doxie says proudly, "I gotta' get down to the studio at KPCE."

"Station KPCE is right on," insists Doobie.

"Yeah," says Doxie. "I have an interview with Jerry Nutter. You may have heard of him. He's pretty famous. He met Janis Joplin. Then she died."

"Wait a second. Do you mean Jerry Nutter at Night?" asks Socrates as if the radio station is filled with 523 guys named Jerry Nutter and the possibility for confusion is immense.

"The one and the same, man," confirms Doxie.

"Groovy," says Doobie.

"Right on," says Socrates.

"Heavy," says Moonbeam.

"Yeah," agrees Doxie. "Hey, now you kids stay in school. School is cool. So be cool and stay in school. Got it?"

"We were expelled," says Doobie.

"We forgot to go for, like, a month," explains Socrates.

"Or three," agrees Moonbeam.

"We forgot," reiterated Doobie. "So it's not really our fault."

"Well," says Doxie, not really knowing what to say. "Stay cool, then."

"We will," chime Doobie, Socrates and Moonbeam in perfect harmony.

"See you later," says Doxie as he begins to walk out to his car.

"Hey," shouts Socrates, stopping Doxie in his tracks. "When is your next gig, man?"

"Whenever I can get the bread together to get a new guitar, I'll do another show," promises Doxie.

"Right on!" says Socrates, thrusting his right fist into the air.

"Later on, then," says Doxie with finality.

"Later on," says Doobie. "Bye little Woodstock."

Doxie quickly turns in his tracks and glares at Doobie sternly.

"I mean, Peabody 18," says Doobie, feeling slightly intimidated.

Alvin wags his tail. Doxie gives Doobie, Socrates and Moonbeam the "thumbs up" signal. Doobie and Socrates and Moonbeam begin to walk away as Doxie walks over to his car.

"Hello, little Peabody 18," Doxie coos to Alvin and he walks over to the passenger's side of his rusted Yugo. Doxie opens the door, crawls in, and places Alvin in the passenger's seat. Doxie straightens his jacket, and with his usual amount of tremendous effort and fighting the steering wheel the entire time, climbs in.

Doxie opens the glove compartment and pulls out a half-melted candy bar. He opens the packaging and, smearing melted chocolate on his hands and face, eats the whole candy bar in one bite, saving a tiny piece for Alvin. He offers the piece to Alvin, but, still full from eating the Powerball ticket, Alvin declines. Doxie eats the last piece, starts the car, and drives away, throwing the candy wrapper out the window.

Alvin wags his tail.

CHAPTER XIV

Doxie's car speeds out of the parking lot of Rock 'N Ho's. His tires squeal as he rounds the corner of the block and directly into the drive-thru of Bob's Wings 'N Things.

Bob's Wings 'N Things has the brightest sign in Midland City. It is four stories high and depicts a buffalo with wings and a giant, animatronic meat cleaver. Every ten seconds, the cleaver cleaves off the wings and blood spurts from the buffalo's shoulders. The blood is collected in a large trough and cycled through and pumped back up through the sign to be used again. Bob thought that this was the cleverest sign in the whole world when he had it built, but the electricity that it takes to run it has nearly put him in bankruptcy eleven times. Bob doesn't care, though. He still thinks that having the biggest sign in all of Midland City is the coolest thing that can happen to him in his lifetime. It's his legacy to mankind. It makes him feel like a "big man." He is going to have a miniature buffalo and cleaver sign constructed for his tombstone.

Doxie pulls up to the drive-thru intercom system, aglow with the lights illuminating the adjacent menu. The menu consists of over 120 available flavors of wings ranging from original flavor to zucchini chocolate mango smoked almond. And each of those flavors is available in extra extra mild, extra mild, mild, medium, extra medium, hot, extra hot, extra extra hot, fire, and unimaginably hot. Doxie studies the menu with great concentration. He is a slow reader. Finally, Doxie has made his decision.

While he was making up her mind, three cars pulled in behind him in the dive-thru line.

"Hello?" says Doxie towards the intercom box.

"Hello?" says the voice from the intercom box.

"Hello?" says Doxie.

"Hello?" says the box.

"Hello?" says Doxie. "I'd like to place an order, please."

More cars pull into the drive-thru line.

"Oh. Okay, then. Hello. Welcome to Bob's Wings 'N Things. What may I prepare especially for you?" says the box.

"I'd like," says Doxie, now unsure of what he wants. "I'd like...I need...I'd like..."

"Yes?" says the box.

More cars pull into the drive-thru line.

"I'd like...I need..." Doxie stammers, his mind agog with the millions of possible combinations that he could choose for dinner.

"Yes?" says the box.

"I'd like...ummm...I want..." Doxie says. "I'd like...hmmmmmmm...How about..."

More cars pull into the drive-thru line behind Doxie.

"Yes?" says the box.

Doxie has been thinking about this meal for two days. He was going to reward himself for performing his gig by trying something new. A new flavor combination. But, now, feeling totally overwhelmed by the choices, and on the verge of a panic attack, Doxie suddenly reverts to his usual selection.

"I want a 72 piece bucket of original mild wings, three jumbo fries, an order of 15 mozzarella sticks, and a super-giant diet root beer, and...uh...and...that'll do it," says Doxie with conviction.

"Do you want any celery sticks with that?" asks the box.

"No thanks," says Doxie.

More cars pull into the drive-thru line. The line now extends well into the street and halfway down the block.

"That'll be 162 dollars and 28 cents at the window," says the box.

"Okay," says Doxie, already knowing that it will be $162.28. It's always $162.28.

Doxie pulls forward, rounding the corner to the window where he is to pay for, and eventually pick up, his food. However, Doxie slams on the brakes and Alvin nearly comes tumbling to the floor of the car as a staggering Trent unexpectedly crosses into their path. Trent is bleeding profusely and has been stumbling and bumbling around Midland City for over an hour. Trent has a major concussion and has lost an amazing amount of blood. He looks like he came directly out of a horror film.

"Watch out, man!" shouts Doxie with much more disdain than concern.

"Have you seen my dog?" cries Trent.

"What dog? What are you talking about?"

"I lost my dog," whimpers Trent in utter despair, tears streaming down his face.

"Does it have a name?" asks Doxie.

"Lucky," gushes Trent. "His name is Lucky!"

"What does he look like?" asks Doxie.

"He is a little dachshund. He is small and black with some white and his eyes look all-weird like he is blind and he is old and...and..." stammers Trent. "He is Lucky, the lucky little dachshund."

Trent sobs. Alvin looks up at Doxie, much of the chemical fire extinguisher dust having rubbed off on the seat of the Yugo, and wags his tail. Doxie looks down at Alvin. A horrible thought goes through Doxie's brain. "What if Peabody 18 actually belongs to this lunatic?" Doxie totally clears his mind just in case the crazy man can read his thoughts. Doxie starts to have a panic attack.

But then Doxie stops freaking out. He boldly determines that even if this is Trent's dog, he is in no shape to care for it. Doxie makes an executive decision. Part of the decision is born from good intentions, the other from a very destructive mental illness that can make an otherwise meek individual quite brave, brash, bold and cunning.

Doxie takes a blanket from the floor of his car and covers Alvin with it. Alvin's wagging tail makes the blanket move to and fro.

"No, sir, I can assure you," says Doxie. "I have not seen your dog."

"I think that he may have my Powerball lottery ticket!" sobs Trent.

"Dogs aren't allowed to play the lottery, sir," Doxie tries to explain to Trent.

"He took my ticket!!!" screams Trent.

"What?"

"He teased me with unimaginable fortune, then he just pulled the rug out from beneath me! I need to find my dog!!!"

"Oh, okay," says Doxie. "That's...okay...whatever."

"I need to find my dog!" Trent yells to the world.

"Well, good luck with that," says Doxie.

"Lucky! Lucky!" shouts Trent, stumbling off towards the parking lot of Rock 'N Ho's.

"Weirdo," mummers Doxie.

Doxie takes the blanket off of Alvin. Alvin continues to wag his tail. Doxie pulls forward to the drive-thru window.

"That'll be $162.28," says Steve, the voice from the drive-thru intercom box. "Oh, hi Doxie."

"Hi Steve," says Doxie.

Doxie is jealous of Steve. He knows that Steve gets a 20 percent discount on food from Bob's Wings 'N Things for being the assistant manager. Doxie would give his left arm to get a 20 percent discount at Bob's Wings 'N Things. Steve is jealous of Doxie, because Doxie knows how to play the guitar. Steve has always wanted to learn how to play the guitar. But he's really, really lazy. He's also missing his left hand. He stuck it out of the school bus window during a field trip to the zoo in fifth grade. The rest is history.

Regardless of their own issues, Doxie and Steve maintain a working relationship. They have never let their deep-seated jealousy for each other ever show. Ever.

"Sorry," apologizes Steve. "I didn't know it was you. How are you doing, Doxie?"

"Okay," says Doxie. "I had a gig tonight."

"That's cool," says Steve cheerily, even though a cauldron of unrest is burning in his belly.

Steve hands Doxie two large bags of food, a giant bucket of wings, and the massive diet soda. The soda takes Doxie both hands to hold on to, although Steve expertly managed it with just one. This burns Doxie to his core. Doxie rests it between his feet and balances it with his shins. This diet root beer, like every drink that Doxie orders, is far, far too large for the cup holder in his car. Doxie has thought about purchasing a larger cup holder, but has never gotten around to it.

"You been busy tonight?" asks Doxie.

"No," laments Steve. "It's been totally dead."

Doxie is uneasy. He knows exactly what he would be doing if he were the assistant manager and it was a slow night at Bob's Wing's 'N Things and there was not much going on. He would be eating himself into a blissful buffalo wing coma. He wonders exactly how many wings that woul take. Steve is anxious. He wonders if he would gain all of Doxie's guitar-playing expertise if he killed him and ate his brain. They both wonder. And they both seethe in total silence for five, excruciating minutes.

"Right on," says Doxie, finally. "Well, take it easy."

"You too, Doxie," says Steve, promising himself for the hundredth time that he will go home tonight and learn how to play the guitar from lessons that he downloaded off the internet on how to play the guitar with only one hand. And, for the hundredth time, he won't. Instead, he'll watch Gilligan's Island re-runs on TV.

Doxie pulls away, opening the bucket of wings and preparing for an unabashed feeding frenzy. The line for the drive-thru now nearly a mile long, Steve is about to have a very busy night. Alvin wags his tail.

CHAPTER XV

Doxie's car pulls into the parking lot of KPCE Radio. He has never been here before, but he knows that he is in the right place because of the flashing "KPCE Radio" sign illuminating the front of the old, red brick building. There is a large, rainbow colored peace sign on both sides of the lettering. The rainbow colors have faded dramatically over the years from exposure to UV rays. And the KPCE Radio sign shouldn't be flashing. It's a major fire hazard.

Doxie is throwing half-eaten chicken wing bones out of the car window. He has left a trail of them all the way from Bob's Wing's 'N Things. Doxie parks right out front and, with both hands, lifts his cup of diet root beer and takes a big, long drink.

Doxie looks at his watch. He is five minutes early. Time enough to eat about 20 wings and one of his containers of french fries and maybe some mozzarella sticks if he hurries. Doxie eats ravenously.

Inside the building, Jerry Nutter sits at his microphone in the studio. The studio is very small and the walls are plastered with posters of Janis Joplin. It looks even smaller than it is because the floors are covered with vinyl records stacked and ordered and arranged in a fashion that only Jerry knows. KPCE is the only radio station in town that still plays vinyl records, and Jerry is incredibly proud of this. On October 30th back in 1976, his boss brought in an 8-track cassette to play, and Jerry had a nervous breakdown. He cried for over two hours and threatened to slash his wrists. Technological upgrades have never been offered again.

Jerry is a very slight man; four feet ten inches tall if he stands on his tippy-toes. And he weighs no more than 90 pounds on a full stomach. He is balding on the very top of his head, but he has let the sides and back grow out for the past 40 years. The thin, grey hair that he has left reaches down past his waist. Jerry is wearing his customary tie-dye T-shirt, cut-off jeans, and brown sandals. Jerry looks old and worn and haggard, because he is, and his face is wrinkled like a prune that has been left in the sun on Mars. Jerry has a giant mole on the very tip of his nose. Jerry has a face that is perfect for the radio.

Jerry's boss, Andre, the station manager, is waiting for Jerry on the other side of the glass door that leads to the studio. Andre is wearing his customary grey pin-striped suit and looks impatiently at his gold and diamond encrusted wristwatch. His black hair is short and neat. His Moroccan leather shoes glow with a perfect shine. This is Andre's third week at KPCE. The old station manager quit the radio business altogether and went back to his old job as a guard at San Quentin Prison in California. Jerry Nutter at Night was just too much for him to deal with.

Jerry sees Andre, but pays him no mind. The red "On Air" light is on, and whenever that is on, Jerry's focus is solely on the microphone so he can connect directly and more personally with his droves of adoring fans.

"And that's when I decided that if I cut my hair for 'the man,' I would just be helpin' Nixon kill babies," Jerry explains to the microphone and, presumably, his audience. "Anyway, I'm gonna' lay some Janis Joplin on you right now, here at KPCE. K-PEACE, where the 60's never die. Ever."

Jerry pushes a button on the console, the record spins, and nothing happens. Jerry pushes more buttons. Nothing happens. Jerry slaps the console frantically with his child-like hands and "Mercedes Benz" by Janis Joplin finally begins to play. The red "On Air" light goes off and Andre opens the glass door and comes into the studio, stepping gingerly over the piles and piles of records that litter the floor.

"Jerry," says Andre, with all the seriousness of a station manager. "We need to talk."

"Not now, man," says Jerry, "I'm in the middle of my show. Can't it wait until after?"

"No," says Andre firmly. "We need to talk right now, and then I am going to go home. I have a wife and family, you know. I want to go home and see them. Be with them. Engage with them. I have a life outside of here."

"I'm gettin' an ugly vibe from you, man," says Jerry, a little worried about the fact that Andre has a life outside of radio. Jerry can't comprehend such a thing.

"And it's about to get uglier," assures Andre. "It's about to get a lot uglier."

"Oh, no," says Jerry. "Take a chill pill, man."

Jerry searches his pockets and finds what he believes to be a "chill pill." In fact, it is a Tic Tac. Wintergreen flavor. He offers it to Andre.

"I will NOT take a chill pill, Jerry," says Andre. "Instead, I will be blunt. I will be blunt, frank, and to the point. We need to make some changes around here, Jerry."

"What kind of changes?" asks Jerry, putting the Tic Tac in his mouth.

"We need some damn ratings," says Andre, being blunt, frank and to the point. Just like he said he would. Andre is a man of his word.

"I get ratings, man," says Jerry, fully convinced that he does, indeed, get ratings. "I work my butt off day in and day out, and I get ratings. My fans love me, man."

"No," corrects Andre. "You tell your 'I met Janis Joplin' story every 15 minutes. That does not draw people into the show. As a matter of fact, it probably drives them away."

"But I DID meet Janis, man!" insists Jerry. "Do you think that I am lying? I didn't make it up, man! I'm telling the truth! I really met her!"

"Okay," sighs Andre. "Here is the bottom line. The quarterly report came out today. The ratings. What we base our success on. How we measure our value. What allows us to charge advertisers so that they will pay us and we can afford to be on the air. So we can stay in business. So we can eat and have a roof over our heads. So we can survive. And do you know what we got for your show, Jerry? We got a grand total of zero for your show. Zero, Jerry. That is one less than one, and one more than a negative one."

"Well," contemplates Jerry, "at least I got more than a negative one. I'm cool with that."

"There is no such thing as a negative one in regards to radio listenership totals," says Andre.

"What are you telling me man? What does that mean? If there is no negative one?" asks Jerry, frightened.

"That means none, Jerry," says Andre firmly. "Nobody listens to your show."

"Nobody?" says Jerry sadly, taking it all in. "Oh, man. Bummer."

"Yeah," agrees Andre. "Killer bummer. It would be cheaper for this station to play static rather than have your show on the air."

"You're bringin' me down, bro'," says Jerry. "What are we going to do?"

"Well," admits Andre, "I'm considering playing static. I really am. Or maybe I'll just play Mayan flute music 24 hours a day, seven days a week. It's a toss-up between the two at this point."

"That'd be cool," says Jerry with excitement and animation. "Mayan flute music is right on, man! It is totally right on!"

"I'm just joking," says Andre. "I would NOT play Mayan flute music. I would just play static."

"That's not right, man," says Jerry, his expression again becoming depressed and worried.

"That's just like paying the farmers not to grow any crops."

"We're not talking about crops, Jerry," says Andre. "And it's not at all like paying farmers to not grow crops. When I play static, Jerry, I will not pay you."

"That's wrong!" says Jerry, suddenly getting very emotional. "Paying money for no crops is WRONG!"

"This isn't about crops," interrupts Andre.

"It IS about crops!" shouts Jerry.

"No," says Andre, calmly. "It is not. It has nothing to do with crops."

"It's always about the crops, man!" insists Jerry. "What with all the hunger in the world today..."

"Are you listening to me?" asks Andre, fearing that his has lost Jerry to his own, bizarre, conversation.

"There are little kids starving to death man! Right now! All over the world!" shouts Jerry.

"What does this have to do with the ratings?" asks Andre.

"There are little babies with flies on their eyes, man!" shouts Jerry.

"Jerry-" interrupts Andre, again. But it is too late. He has lost him. The switch has been thrown. Jerry is unreachable. The conversation, for all intents and purposes, is over.

"Flies on their eyes!" shouts Jerry. "And none of you 'suits' care about the little babies, man!"

"I'm leaving now," says Andre with exasperation.

"Oh, God," sobs Jerry. "The HUMANITY!"

"I'll see you tomorrow and we can talk about this then," says Andre.

"The HUMANITY!!!" cries Jerry, burying his face in his hands and sobbing uncontrollably.

Andre shakes his head, looks at his watch, and leaves the studio. As Andre is passing through the door, exiting the studio, Doxie and Alvin come in to the studio. Doxie is carrying Alvin under his left arm, and he carries his three quarters empty bucket of chicken wings under his right arm. Doxie has chicken wing sauce all over his face and shirt. Doxie and Andre exchange glances, but don't say a word. Andre closes the door behind Doxie, and Doxie walks over to Jerry, being careful not to step on any records.

"Are you okay?" Doxie asks Jerry.

"Huh?" says Jerry, as if coming out of a trance. "Oh, yeah, man. I'm okay. The state of the world was getting me down for a minute there, but I'm okay now."

Jerry wipes the tears from his eyes and blows his nose on the sleeve of his T-shirt.

"Are you Jerry Nutter? Jerry Nutter at Night?" asks Doxie excitedly.

"Yeah, man. And you must be Jimi Hendrix."

"Yep," says Doxie with pride.

"Cute dog, man," says Jerry, indicating Alvin. "What's its name?"

"His name is Peabody 18," says Doxie.

"Peabody," repeats Jerry.

"18," finishes Doxie.

"Right on," says Jerry.

"Right on," says Doxie.

"Pets, man," says Jerry, nodding. "They are a wonderful creation. They give you that unconditional love. Everybody needs that unconditional love. You gotta' dig it, man."

"Right on," agrees Doxie, shifting Alvin so that he can hold Alvin and the bucket of chicken wings with one hand. Doxie reaches into the bucket and fondles the chicken wings. He is in heaven.

"I know all about that man. The love," explains Jerry. "I have a hermit crab. I painted her shell with the peace sign, man. Her name is Janis."

"Janis," says Doxie. "I can dig it."

"Are you ready for your interview, man?" asks Jerry, looking up at the clock.

"Yeah, man," says Doxie. "Let's do it. Do you want a chicken wing?" offers Doxie.

"No thanks, man," says Jerry. "I'm a vegan."

"Heavy," says Doxie, pulling out and eating two chicken wings at once. "You have some major convictions, man."

"Right on, man," says Jerry, appreciating the compliment. "Well, it's convictions, and it's also the fact that animal fat gives me violent, explosive diarrhea."

"Bummer, man," says Doxie, eating another one of the chicken wings and throwing the bone back into the bucket.

"Yeah," says Jerry, "I learned that one the hard way. Anyway, you just sit right there in that chair there, and talk right into the microphone in front of you."

Jerry indicates the chair and the microphone.

"Should I talk louder?" asks Doxie. "So the people can hear me? Since some people may have the volume on their radios turned down?"

"No, man," explains Jerry. "My audience always has the volume cranked up to 11 so they can 'rock out'! We won't have any volume control issues, man, so just talk in your regular speaking voice."

"Right on," says Doxie, eating another chicken wing.

Doxie sits down in the chair and the chair groans underneath his bulk. He puts Alvin on the table next to the microphone. Alvin looks at the microphone. Alvin wags his tail. Doxie puts the nearly empty bucket of chicken wings next to Alvin. Jerry fades out the song, pushes a button, and he is back on the air. The red "On Air" sign lights up.

"Okay, people," Jerry says to the microphone. "I've got a special guest for you tonight. Right here, in this very studio, I have, with me, live, and in person, the one and only, Jimi Hendrix."

"Hi Jerry," says Doxie, talking slightly louder than usual even though he was told not to. Doxie waves at the microphone, not fully grasping the concept of radio. "Hi everybody."

"So," says Jerry, making eye contact with Doxie. "You're coming here fresh from a gig tonight at Rock 'N Ho's. How did that go for you, man? Was it groovin'?"

"You bet man," says Doxie.

"How was the crowd, man?" asks Jerry.

"It was wild," laughs Doxie. "It was awesome. There were tons of people. I have a much larger fan base then I thought. I was surprised. Shocked, really. Just incredible. And totally, totally crazy!"

"Lots of groupies, eh?" laughs Jerry.

"Lots of groupies," laughs Doxie. "Men, women, children...dogs, cats, owls. I'm so popular I don't know what to do!"

"Right on!" shouts Jerry.

"My fans love me," says Doxie.

"Good for you, man!" exclaims Jerry with envy.

"I'm beating them off with a stick, man," says Doxie.

"No man!" shouts Jerry with horror. "Don't beat 'em off, man! Free love! Free love!"

Doxie gets a very serious look on his face. Doxie looks down at the floor. Doxie clears his throat.

"Free love only gets you so far, man," confides Doxie, lowering his voice. "When you are so totally hot, like I am, and you got the talent, well, they want you day and night. And it gets old. It gets really old, man. People pulling you ten different directions at once. It makes it tough to keep your head straight."

Jerry ponders this.

"That reminds me of a story," says Jerry. "Can I tell you a story?"

"Okay," says Doxie, leaning back in his chair with a container of deep-fried mozzarella sticks and making himself comfortable. Doxie listens with anticipation.

"Did you know that I met Janis Joplin?" asks Jerry.

"I think I heard you mention it once or twice on your show," says Doxie.

"Do you mind if I re-cap?" asks Jerry.

"Not at all," assures Doxie, intrigued.

"I think that the story has some particular pertinence to what you just said," says Jerry.

"Okay," says Doxie, reaching for another chicken wing. "Lay it on me."

"I met Janis in the parking lot of the Winterland Ballroom on April 13th, 1968," begins Jerry.

"Groovy," says Doxie, stuffing chicken wings and mozzarella sticks in his mouth at the same time.

"So, anyway, I'm in the parking lot and Janis walks up to my van. I was really stoked. I said, 'Hi, Janis. How you doin', man?' And she said, 'I'm selling my heart, man. I'm selling my heart.' And I was all, like, 'Heavy.' And she was all, like, 'Do you have any Southern Comfort?' And I said, 'No.' And then she threw up on my shoe. Just two years later, and she was dead. I didn't have any Southern Comfort, then she died. I gotta' be honest with you, Doxie. It was heavy. We're talkin' really heavy, man. Really, really heavy."

"Heavy," agrees Doxie.

"I still have the shoe," says Jerry with a tone that insinuates that the shoe imposes some kind of burden on him.

"Wow," exclaims Doxie.

"Do you want to see it?" asks Jerry.

"What?" says Doxie. "Right now?"

"Yes. The shoe. I have it here," says Jerry. "I keep it in my locker here at the station."

"No thanks, man," says Doxie. "Maybe later. After the interview."

"Sure," says Jerry, feeling a little hurt. "Right on, man. Hey, do you have any Southern Comfort, Jimi?"

"No," says Doxie.

"Me either," says Jerry. "And now Janis is dead."

"That's amazing, man," agrees Doxie.

"I know," states Jerry. "But, getting back to the point I wanted to make, do you think that you are selling your heart, Jimi?"

"Well," explains Doxie. "In a way, yes. But, I mean, it's kind of my job. I do my music for me, but I also do it for my fans. I have hit that point in my career where it is no longer only about doing it for me. For my soul. Which was healthy, man. It was really healthy. But now I have to do it for other people, man. I can only imagine that all of my fans would kill themselves if I stopped playing music. There would be such an emptiness...a complete and utter void in their lives that they would just have to end it all. Mass suicide. And I don't want to be responsible for that, man. I don't. But I guess that's the price you pay when you are an entertainer."

"That's deep, man," says Jerry. "Deep. So how did you get involved with music?"

"I just like music," explains Doxie. "I always have. I think, actually, that a lot of people like music. It's not just me. I talk with my Mommy about this all the time. She says that my love of music, and of rock and roll, and my talent when it comes to music, is a gift from God. But, sometimes, I feel like it is more of a curse than a gift. Or a burden. No. Wait. A curse. It is definitely a curse. Or both. Yeah. It's both. It's a hybrid. I guess you could call it a 'burse' that should have been a gift."

"Oh wow, man," says Jerry. "Heavy."

"I know," agrees Doxie.

"So," says Jerry, "I have to ask you one question that I have been dying to know the answer to. Are you...Jimi Hendrix?"

"Yes," says Doxie, emphatically.

"No," says Jerry, clarifying, "I mean, the REAL Jimi Hendrix."

"Absolutely," says Doxie with certainty.

"Okay," says Jerry. "But, two things here. They may be a stretch, so you'll have to just sort of go with me on this..."

"I'm with 'ya, Jerry!"

"Okay. Point number one, Jimi Hendrix was black. And you are white."

"Okay," says Doxie, not quite understanding where Jerry's line of questioning is going.

"And, secondly, Jimi Hendrix died a long time ago."

"Oh," says Doxie. "You know, I get these questions a lot, actually. Anyway, Jimi Hendrix, I'll call him Jimi Hendrix "A," died on September 18th, 1970. I, and we will call me Jimi Hendrix "B," was born on June 18th, 1971. That is exactly nine months later."

"No way," says Jerry, finally getting the heaviness of the thought. "So you're telling me..."

"That I, Jimi Hendrix 'B' am the reincarnation of Jimi Hendrix 'A'."

"You're blowin' my mind, here, Jimi!" shouts Jerry, beginning to freak out a bit.

"I know, man," says Doxie, nodding his head. "It's pretty deep. I know."

"That is sooooo freaky!" shouts Jerry.

"Well, here. Now let me lay this on you. I'm white because my Daddy is Elvis," adds Doxie.

"No way!" screams Jerry, totally freaking out.

"But that is a whole different story, entirely," says Doxie. "I don't think that we have time to go in to it tonight."

"Far out!" shouts Jerry, his mind blown away.

"I know," says Doxie with pride. "I am blessed, man. I am really blessed."

"You are so amazing!" shrieks Jerry.

"I know," says Doxie. "I know."

Doxie, now overflowing with the sin of pride, takes a chicken wing out of the bucket and begins to eat it. Doxie always eats too fast when he is overflowing with the sin of pride. With the sin of anything, actually. But, for Doxie, the sin of pride usually leads to the sin of gluttony. And that usually leads to some kind of disaster.

"No doubt you are blessed, man!" shouts Jerry. "No doubt! Wow! I am in the presence of greatness!"

Jerry buries his head in his hands in excitement, and turns away from Doxie to look at the Janis posters on the wall. Tears well up in Jerry's eyes. Jerry contemplates how lucky he is to have his job and to be able to meet the people he meets. Doxie begins to choke on the chicken wing that he has, literally, inhaled. Alvin wags his tail. Jerry talks into the side of the microphone while staring longingly at his Janis posters, oblivious to Doxie's plight.

"My astrologer, Mythica Sunshine," begins Jerry, "she said that I would have a brush with greatness today, and she was right, man! She nailed it! She was right on!"

Doxie continues to choke and quickly comes to the realization that he is in trouble. This has happened to him before, and it literally scares the crap out of him every time. But it doesn't scare him enough to make him be more careful. Doxie tries to get Jerry's attention, but Jerry is in his own little world right now. Doxie tries to give himself the Heimlich maneuver. Doxie is now choking quite badly and unable to make a sound. Alvin continues to wag his tail.

"I thought that she just meant it metaphorically," continues a totally self-absorbed Jerry, "but I should have taken it literally. Mythica Sunshine is always right, man. She is always right. Have you ever done that, Jimi? Where you take something that somebody says one way, when you should have taken it a whole completely different way? Jimi? Jimi?"

Doxie falls to the floor, unable to breathe. Doxie clutches his throat and flops around like a beached whale. Alvin wags his tail. Doxie starts to poop his pants. Jerry finally snaps out of it and notices that Doxie is choking to death.

"Oh my God!" shouts Jerry. "Jimi!"

Jerry runs over to Doxie. Doxie's face quickly turns a deep shade of purple. Jerry, with all of his weakling might, pounds on Doxie's chest as hard as he can, but to no avail. Jerry couldn't squish a fly, let alone dislodge a chicken bone from someone's throat. Beginning to panic, and not knowing what to do, Jerry jumps up and down on Doxie's chest.

"Hang in there, Jimi! Don't die like Janis!" pleads Jerry. "I couldn't handle another death!"

Jerry continues to jump on Doxie's chest. Doxie's eyes are beginning to roll back into his head. Jerry realizes that he needs more weight to force the bone out of Doxie's throat. Jerry picks up Alvin, and, carefully holding him with both hands, jumps up and down on Doxie's chest some more. Alvin wags his tail and barks. Alvin likes bouncing up and down. It is almost as much fun as "rocking out." It is all very exciting.

As it turns out, Jerry is right. The extra seven pounds of Alvin's body weight is just what he needs to remedy the situation. The chicken bone flies out of Doxie's mouth and hits the ceiling. The bone falls back down to earth and lands in the bucket. Doxie begins to breathe again.

"Oh, thank God," says Jerry, beginning to cry. "Thank God."

Doxie lays motionless on the floor and, being mindful of his piles of records, Jerry does a little hopscotch routine to the telephone to call an ambulance. Jerry looks back at Doxie.

"I'm glad you didn't die, Janis," says Jerry.

Doxie considers correcting Jerry, but instead concentrates on breathing.

CHAPTER XVI

Outside the front door of the KPCE radio station, Jerry trembles as he clutches a tail-wagging Alvin. They both watch as Doxie rolls on a gurney towards the ambulance, which has been backed up onto the sidewalk. The paramedic and the ambulance driver strain, groan, and otherwise have a difficult time pushing Doxie to the ambulance on the gurney. They don't mind too much, though, as by comparison they had an even more difficult time loading Doxie onto the gurney in the tiny studio. Doxie was total dead weight. The paramedic and ambulance driver had to use two pieces of lumber and a couple of cinder blocks that they found at the construction site next door to lever him up onto the gurney. They had to use the laws of physics to their advantage. Which they did. However, overall, the extraction didn't go very smoothly and it took a lot longer than it should have.

"This is Jimi's dog, Peabody 18," says Jerry, offering Alvin to them.

"We can't take the dog to the hospital, sir," grunts the paramedic.

For the paramedic, the extraction of Doxie went especially poorly. The paramedic is angry. He thinks that Doxie has given him a hernia. Even though workman's compensation insurance will cover the cost of his surgery and recovery, he dreads the fact that his co-workers will make fun of him for hurting himself by lifting a fat man with his stomach muscles rather than with his leg muscles. He can't stand that thought. He failed something that they teach you in paramedic 101 class. He feels like an idiot, and he is in a lot of pain. That's because he did a lot more than get an intestine-pinching hernia. He also ruptured his spleen and one of his kidneys. His good kidney, as it turns out. The paramedic will never forget this night.

None of this matters to Jerry. He does not know what to do with Alvin. That's his singular concern right now.

"What do you want me to do with Peabody 18?" Jerry asks Doxie as he rolls by.

Doxie looks at Jerry. Doxie raises one arm with great difficulty.

"Uhhhhhgggggghhhhhh..." murmurs Doxie.

Doxie drops his arm and is unconscious. The paramedic and ambulance driver load him into the ambulance with a mighty grunt and a mighty groan. The driver runs around and gets in the front while the paramedic, holding his side where his intestines are poking through his stomach muscles, climbs in the back with Doxie and closes the doors. The ambulance pulls off, lights flashing and siren wailing. Not so much for Doxie, but for the paramedic who will need to have emergency hernia surgery within the hour or else he will die. Alvin wags his tail. Jerry looks at his wristwatch.

"Well," says Jerry, "Peabody 18, I have to get going. It looks like you are going to have to come with me."

Jerry has put a stack of thirty records on the turntable to play in succession at the radio station that will go out over the airwaves, just like he does every night at this time, to cover for the fact that he is not there. Jerry locks the front door and begins his nightly walk to the Sir William Old Folks' Home. It takes Jerry half an hour to get there. Jerry looks at his wristwatch again. It is nine seconds later than it was when he looked before.

"Oh no! We gotta' run or I'm gonna' be late," Jerry tells Alvin. Jerry has a horrible sense of time. He also has a very loose definition of 'running.'

Alvin wags his tail.

"Where? The Sir William Old Folks' Home. It's the court ordered community service I have to do. Three hours a night, seven days a week, for the next year and a half. I got pulled over last year. The cop said that I was stoned. I wasn't, but he thought I was. It's probably because of my long hair. Cops don't like you if you have long hair. He wanted to do a blood test on me, but I said 'No way, man. The government isn't getting any of my blood. The government has taken the blood of too many innocent people as it is, man! Stop harassin' me, man! Just back off, Mister Bad Vibe Cop Dude Just BACK OFF!' So he didn't like hearin' that one bit and arrested me and I had to go to court. Let me tell you one thing, Peabody 18, if you ever have to go to court, you probably shouldn't put on a blindfold and go in and announce that 'Justice is Blind.' The judge didn't think that was very cool. Even if it is true, which it is, they'll throw the book at you. It's a bum rap, man. I got a bum rap. Because we live in a state of tyranny, man. It's so uncool..."

Jerry gets sad, thinking about how he was screwed over by the system. He drifts into deep thought. Jerry is bummed out. Jerry hates to be bummed out, which bums him out even more. Jerry is in danger of plummeting into a bummer-spiral of sadness. And this makes Jerry even MORE bummed out. Jerry's brain is lost is a complex matrix of bummin' vibes. Jerry walks.

CHAPTER XVII

Jerry slowly dawdles, in his own typical meandering Jerry Nutter at Night fashion, thinking about how he was screwed over by the system. He drifts deep into thought. Jerry is bummed out. Jerry hates to be bummed out because knowing he's bummed out bums him out even more. Jerry is in danger of plummeting into a bummer-spiral of sadness. This makes Jerry even MORE bummed out. Jerry's brain is lost is a complex matrix of bummin'. Jerry toddles right by George and Ralph without paying them any notice. Nor they to him and Alvin. It's the time of night when people don't engage in the affairs of others by acknowledging that they exist.

George and Ralph are at the bus stop. Ralph clutches the case of vodka like a baby and George is finishing off the last of the peanut butter and jelly sandwiches. They are in bliss.

"So where are we going, Ralph?" George asks, for the 30th time in 90 seconds.

"To the bus station," says Ralph with measured patience. "We are taking the local bus from the bus stop to the big bus station so that we can take a national bus and get out of here."

"Why, Ralph?" says George. "I thought that we were going to go and have a bath and sleep on a real bed."

"We need to go away from here, George," says Ralph. "Life is like a chicken ladder. Short and full of crap. We need a new ladder, George. One with less crap on it. We have two hundred dollars to our name. That is one hundred dollars each. Remember how much we had when we got to Midland City? We didn't have a single penny between us. And we got lucky and hit it big. And the rule is that when you hit it big, you gotta' walk away from the table or else you're just gonna' lose it all. We are leaving Midland City rich men, George. If we stay, we're just gonna' lose it all."

"Yes," says George, "One hundred dollars each. But where are we going to go?"

"One hundred dollars' worth of 'away from here,' George, and we won't know exactly where that is until we get to the bus station and ask" says Ralph. "But I'm guessin' that one hundred dollars' worth could be a long, long ways. The bus can take you halfway across the country for a hundred dollars. That's because they deal in volume."

"Can we go someplace warm, Ralph?" asks George. "I'd sure like to go someplace where it's warm."

"Yes we can, George" says Ralph, patting George's hand. "We will."

Ralph smiles. George smiles. George waits for the bus to take them to the bus station. He is content.

Without any warning, Trent wanders loudly and clumsily from out behind the bushes. His head and face is caked with blood, although he had mopped most of it off with his shirt, which, at this point in Trent's journey, is long gone. His pants are ripped and torn. He looks like hell and his brain is still quite fuzzy from the concussion.

"Have you seen my dog?" asks Trent, not recognizing George and Ralph from outside the liquor store.

"No," says Ralph, not recognizing Trent, either. "We have not."

"Damn," says Trent, slinking down and sitting next to George.

"Are you okay, Mister?" asks George.

"I lost my dog," laments Trent.

"I had a dog," offers George. "I miss him."

"I miss mine, too," says Trent.

"My dog is gone forever," says George.

"So's mine," says Trent, finally accepting that he's not going to find Alvin and that he's just not going to win. Ever. So maybe he should just cut himself some slack and just stop trying.

"Hey, do you want a drink?" offers Ralph.

Trent nods "yes" and Ralph hands him one of the bottles of vodka.

Trent drinks down a giant gulp.

"So," says Trent, "where are you guys goin'?"

"We're going someplace warm," says George.

"I want to go someplace, too," says Trent. "I need to get out of here. Run away. I'd say that my life is ruined, but that would imply that it was, at some point, in good shape."

"Don't you got any place to go?" asks George.

"I have a home. Well, a roof over my head. Yeah. But I don't think I can go back there anymore. My wife is going to kill me. I lost another job. She told me that if I lost one more job, I shouldn't come home. Ever again. Which, you know, makes sense because since I lost my job, we can't pay the mortgage so the bank is going to foreclose on us and take the house and my wife and son will move in with her parents and I'm pretty sure that I'm not going to be too welcome there. So, actually, I'm homeless."

"Boy," says Ralph, "That's tough."

"Yeah," agrees Trent. "But you know what? At least I don't have to worry about it anymore. This eventuality has been hovering over my head for years. **YEARS**. And now I don't have to fear it. I don't have to fear the future. It's not going to keep me awake at night and it's not going to give me any more stomach ulcers and it's not going to make me feel like I'm having a heart attack when I wake up every morning. The future is now. It's happening. And what does it actually feel like? It feels like this. This. Here. Right now. And...it's not as bad as I thought. So, in a way, this is all a relief. The fear is gone, at least. That weight has been lifted."

They all drink the gulping vodka in silence and stare off into the distance.

"We're homeless," says George. "It's not so bad. Hey! You know what? We're skipping town tonight! Gonna' get **NEW** lives!"

"A new life," mumbles Trent, never really having considered the endless possibility and potential of it all.

"You wanna' come with us?" quickly offers George, much to the chagrin of Ralph.

"Sure," says Trent. "That is very kind of you to offer. This is all very new to me. Thank you very much."

"Do you have any money?" asks Ralph, considering the practicality of it all.

"No," says Trent, in a lamenting and ashamed tone. "I don't have any money at all."

Ralph's face falls. Now that George invited him, he knows that his 100 dollars each to get away from here has disintegrated into 66 dollars each to get away from here. And there is no way to tactfully un-invite him. Or is there? Ralph ponders...

Suddenly, Trent remembers something. He feels around in his left pants pocket. He pulls out the scratch lottery ticket. Trent looks at the scratch lottery ticket.

"But," says Trent, a broad grin appearing on his face, "I have a winning lottery ticket for five thousand dollars."

Ralph and George look at the ticket. They can't believe their eyes. Ralph isn't entirely sure it's real, but he doesn't care. He's feeling pretty tipsy.

"Well," says Ralph to George and Trent, "it looks like we are going to be able to take the bus anywhere we want."

George giggles with glee. Trent laughs a hearty laugh and Ralph slaps him on the back. Trent is happy to have his new friends. He is happy to have ANY friends. But he's sure happy he got these friends. It's not lost on Trent how Ralph and George accepted him and showed him kindness before they knew he even had any money. They take turns drinking the gulping vodka and smile.

As Ralph takes a long swig, out of the corner of his eye he sees Shane and Jim running very slowly down the sidewalk. They have been running for an hour and a half, ever since the sun went down. They are covered in pigeon feces from head to toe as they were relentlessly pooped upon all afternoon and for the better part of the early evening. Tiny flecks peel and flake off of them as they run. They are white and grey and disgusting. They look like leper ghosts from Hell. Shane hiccups painfully as he runs. But he's alive. They are both alive. And for that, they are immensely grateful.

After what feels like an eternity, they pass by Ralph, George and Trent. Shane and Jim pay them no mind. They are focused on getting out of town. Shane and Jim run. And run. And run.

"They sure are messy," says Trent, finally.

"I'm glad I'm not them," George chimes in.

"I wonder what they are running from," wonders Trent, taking the bottle of vodka from Ralph.

"Maybe they aren't running 'from,' but running 'to'," says George. "Like us."

"I don't know," says Ralph, who is suddenly somewhat drunk. "There are a million stories in this City. And none of them, I repeat, NONE OF THEM, are our business."

George and Trent nod in agreement, and they sit there and wait for the bus in silence. They may not know where they are going, but they all know in their hearts that as long as they stick together, it's all going to be okay. For this, they are immensely grateful.

Tonight, the bus station will be filled with more true gratitude than it's had in years.

CHAPTER XVIII

The ambulance speeds towards Midland City General Hospital. It is only about five minutes away from the radio station, and there's really no traffic to speak of, so the ambulance driver is feeling pretty comfortable about completing his job without incident. He's making awesome time. So awesome, in fact, that he is able to think about things other than driving. Like his grocery list.

The paramedic in the back isn't doing as well. He's not sure if he's going to live, let alone think about what he needs from the store. He doesn't know if he'll see a grocery store ever again. His hernia injury has twisted up his intestines and tweaked a few of his inner organs and that is making him slip in and out of consciousness. He's fighting it, though, with everything he's got. He's determined to keep it together. He wants to be awake and coherent when they get to the hospital so he can make sure to tell his friends who work there to make sure Doxie gets extra sub-par care. He wants to make sure that Doxie's insurance is denied and he has to keep filling out forms until his hand cramps up and that he has to share a room with a total psycho. The paramedic is usually a really nice person, but his major character flaw is that he can become extremely spiteful whenever he's in pain. And he's in a hell of a lot of pain right now.

Doxie is awake and rapidly becoming more coherent by the moment. He is remembering being in the middle of an important interview and he was just totally crushing it when he starts choking on a chicken wing. Then he remembers that he had a dog. He had a dog and now he does not. Moreover, he is in an ambulance. Somewhere in there, Doxie is pretty sure that he must have lost consciousness. Or been abducted by aliens. Or both. The thought of aliens with his dog, possibly doing an anal probe, makes Doxie start to cry.

Now Doxie remembers seeing Jerry Nutter holding the dog as he was loaded into the ambulance. Doxie is not pleased by this image. Instead of being sad, now he's mad. That is HIS dog. All of Doxie's energy immediately goes into plotting about how he is going to get his dog back from that thieving bastard, Jerry Nutter.

Up front, the ambulance driver is oblivious to the plight of his co-worker, so he turns on some country music to help him relax and maybe jog his memory so he can remember what his wife told him to get from the grocery store on the way home from work. He remembers milk, oregano, hamburger buns and corn tortillas. But there was a fifth thing. He knows there was a fifth thing. For the life of him, he can't remember what the heck it is. He thinks it may begin with the letter "s." Was it shampoo? Shallots? Or was it saline solution? He can't ask her, because then she'll know that he wasn't listening and she'll be pissed. But if he gets the wrong thing, she'll know that he wasn't listening and she'll be pissed. The paramedic's wife is emotionally volatile. They've been going to court ordered therapy, but it's not helping. It's a no-win situation. He starts to have a panic attack.

The ambulance driver's train of thought is shattered by the paramedic in the back letting out a bloodcurdling scream of pain. The driver flinches. He falters. He flakes out. The ambulance driver runs the ambulance off the road and into a seven-year-old elm tree that won't live to see eight. Airbags explode from the dashboard and doors, knocking the ambulance driver out. The paramedic is already unconscious, his last utterance being in the form of a bloodcurdling scream of pain. The only occupant of the ambulance who is NOT unconscious is Doxie.

Doxie removes the oxygen mask from his mouth and unstraps himself from the gurney. Stepping over the body of the paramedic, Doxie opens the back door of the ambulance and steps out into the night air.

Doxie is on his way back to **KPCE**. Doxie needs to get his dog back. And he needs to do it now. Nobody steals his dog. No way. No how. Never.

Doxie is certain. The dog will again be his. Destiny wills it. Doxie is positive that everything will work out in his favor.

But Doxie is also certain and positive that's he wearing clothes. He is not. His clothes were literally ripped to shreds while he was being loaded onto the gurney. All Doxie is wearing is a paper-smock...and it's not tied in the back. Right now, most of Doxie's brain is in another universe. The only part existing in reality is the part that needs chicken wings and dachshunds. Lots of wings and wiener dogs.

The fifth thing the ambulance driver's wife wanted him to bring home celery. Which he will. In a week and a half when he's discharged from the hospital.

CHAPTER XIX

The staff of Mister Happy's Super Duper Ole Time Fun Ice Cream Shoppe huddle silently in the corner of the store playing pointless games on their respective phones, waiting patiently for their final customers of the evening to leave. They are sitting at the counter at the front window, and they are taking their time in indulging in Ole Time Fun. The staff, though complacent, is not feeling Super Duper. The staff want to leave, but it's against company policy to make paying customers leave after the posted closing time as long as they are still paying. Mister Happy does not believe in overtime, so the staff has been working for free for almost an hour. Mister Happy has made nine extra dollars in sales during this time.

And, yet, the customers linger. They've been here for nearly two hours. The customers are Guido, Little Anthony and Big Anthony. It's Little Anthony's birthday, and they are celebrating with food. For dinner, they went to Rossi's and had cheese pizza with extra cheese and no sauce. With cheese on the side. Rossi's is one of those restaurants that uses cloth napkins.

Little Anthony has recovered, for the most part, from his horrible allergic reaction. He can breathe, so that makes him happy. He still has some blotches on his skin and they are exaggerated by the fact that they have been smeared with calamine lotion and so they look worse than they are, but the lotion makes him feel a million times better and there's no way that Little Anthony isn't going to wash it off. The doctors at the emergency room were really nice to Little Anthony, and he even got a sucker for being so brave and not dying. They even gave him an EpiPen for when it happens again. Little Anthony lost it before he even got back to the car.

Big Anthony is really angry. He and Guido agreed that they wouldn't get Little Anthony any gifts. They were going to make a donation in Little Anthony's name to the Shriners Hospitals for Children. But right when they were finishing up dinner and the waiter was clearing the plates, Guido pulled out an envelope with a certificate informing Little Anthony that he was now a member of the Stapler of the Month Club. Every month, for the next 12 months, Little Anthony will be receiving a new and fashionable stapler that is not only aesthetically pleasing, but practical as well. Little Anthony was overjoyed to see that the first stapler he would be receiving would be one that's in the shape of a penguin. Little Anthony loves penguins. They make him laugh.

Seething from the betrayal and possibility of losing face and being labeled as a cheap-ass bastard, Big Anthony was forced to pretend to have to use the restroom and instead run outside and procure Little Anthony's gifts from the only other store that was open in the strip mall. Lenny's gas station. Big Anthony gave Little Anthony a keychain that says "Midland City," a pine scented air freshener and an ice scraper. He wrapped them in a map of Midland City. Little Anthony loves them. But Big Anthony is still angry. He has crap at home in a box he likes to use as gifts for "work friends." And, he actually does have to go to the bathroom.

They look out the window and enjoy their ice cream in silence. Even though they are celebrating, they are actually on the clock. They are watching their car, parked across the street. The paint gleans in the moonlight. Big Anthony takes pride in this fact. In front of their car is Moises' car. Both cars are on the street in front of the Sir William Old Folks' Home. Moises said that he had some business to tend to before they go to their meeting tonight. Instead of waiting in their car, like they would usually do, they saw that Mister Happy's was just across the street and they decided to indulge their respective sweet tooths. Which they did. Which Little Anthony still is. He's on his fifth sundae. Which is fine. Moises has been inside across the street forever. They have to leave soon or else they'll be late for their big meeting.

Little Anthony is loving the fact that he can eat himself into an ice cream coma and he wishes that every day was his birthday. Big Anthony is fuming about the breach of gift protocol, but damn proud of how clean he keeps the Mob's Cadillac car. Guido is nervous about how many calories he's going to have to burn off at the gym in the morning, and that Moises has been inside for so long. However, they will all soon gain a singular focus. Right now.

Flashing lights draw their attention to their right. They are coming from around the corner, off in the distance. They are getting closer. Very, very slowly.

Doxie stumbles around the corner and down the street. He is most definitely looking worse for wear. His smock is super-saturated with sweat and it's clinging to his body. Well, what's left of it is clinging to his body. The crotch and under-arm areas were worn off early on in his journey due to extreme chafing. And Doxie's entire back-side is exposed because the actual size of extra extra large is open to interpretation from the manufacturer. Totally driven by acquiring dachshunds and motivated by chicken wings, Doxie is running the best that he can, and it's not good. He needs to get back to the radio studio before someone steals his dog and eats his wings. The thought of those two things happening is just too much to bear. It's like daggers through his soul. The ultimate treachery.

Doxie vows to the universe that if he gets to the radio station, there are no chicken wings, and there is no dog, he will personally kill Jerry Nutter at Night with his own two hands. Then he will kill him again, just for good measure. And then he will burn him. And then dissolve the ashes in acid. Doxie needs more oxygen in his brain. He's not thinking clearly. Doxie's brain is broken. Lucky for Jerry, Doxie will never make it to the radio station. He is running like an extremely overweight drunken toddler.

Doxie had a nice, big burst of energy when he escaped from the ambulance. He had a lot of adrenaline and he was totally focused in regards to his purpose. After a block and a half, Doxie hit the wall. The runner's wall. The runner's wall is a wall that Doxie is not at all familiar with, since he isn't a runner. He certainly wasn't expecting it. Basically, "hitting the wall" is a condition of sudden fatigue and loss of energy which is caused by the depletion of glycogen stores in the liver and muscles. For Doxie, that translates to complete loss of balance and power and, in Doxie's case, rational thought. His energy and adrenaline are gone. He feels lightheaded. Nauseous. Dizzy. Faint. He needs more oxygen. He is so oxygen depleted that he doesn't notice a cop car has been following him for nearly five minutes. It's a K-9 unit, and they are waiting for back-up. The police dog's name is Truman. Not for Harry S. Truman, the 33rd president of the United States. No. For Truman Capote. The eccentric novelist, screenwriter, playwright and actor. Very, very different people. But it doesn't matter to Truman the K-9. He doesn't know, or care, who he's named after. He has his own identity, and he's comfortable with that. As a 185-pound German Shepard in his prime, Truman doesn't feel the need to ever explain anything to anybody. Ever.

Bruno, Little Anthony and Big Anthony don't take as much notice of Doxie as they do the patrol car that rounds the corner behind him. Sure, the mob had bought off the cops, for the most part, but they can attribute the majority of their criminal success in not getting caught in the first place. There can't be a trial if there are never any charges. Also, not everybody in Midland City can be bought. Only half. So, indeed, they still have enemies.

Doxie starts stumbling wildly. He looks like he is going to face-plant himself on the sidewalk at any moment. He doesn't. Somehow, he keeps matriculating forward. Doxie stumbles into the street gutter and falls onto the back of Guido and the Anthony's Cadillac car. He leaves handprints on the trunk and side and he pushes off and tries to propel himself further down the block. This act of sacrilege doesn't please Big Anthony. He wants to go out there right now and wipe off the handprints with his handkerchief and kick the snot out of Doxie for even having the nerve to touch the car to begin with. But he can't. Not with the police as witnesses. Guido senses Big Anthony's fury, and appreciates that he doesn't have to address it.

Doxie pulls himself along the Cadillac and thrusts himself forward onto Moises' Mercedes. Doxie hits the trunk with a mighty *THUD*. Doxie rolls off the trunk of the Mercedes and onto the hood of the Cadillac. This is too much and Big Anthony jumps to his feet. Guido puts a hand on his shoulder to keep him from running out the door and starting an ugly scene. But, it turns out, there was no need for Guido to stop Big Anthony. As Doxie lies motionless on the hood of the Cadillac, the trunk of the Mercedes pops open.

This confuses Doxie. It confuses Guido. It confuses Big Anthony. It does not confuse Little Anthony. He is busy enjoying his ice cream and isn't engaged in the drama unfolding before him. Yet.

It turns out that the trunk popping open is a defect that will lead to the recall of this particular model of Mercedes automobile. It isn't a particularly dangerous defect, and wouldn't necessarily lead to the loss of life. Just to a loss of stuff. So, if anything, it's annoying and possibly expensive. Compared to, say, complete brake failure for no reason, a jolt to the top of the trunk causing it to open isn't a big deal. Unless you have something of value in your trunk or you have something to hide. Or, in this case, both. It turns out to be a fairly ambiguous defect for Doxie as far as how it impacts his long-term future. Not so much for Moises.

Doxie staggers off the hood of the Cadillac as two more police cars arrive on the scene. Sometimes, when people don't feel good, and also depending on the circumstances, they can appear dangerous and threatening when they're really not. Like Doxie is appearing right now. Doxie doesn't have a mean bone in his body, but you won't know it by looking at him. Half naked in the dark shadows, his hospital gown asunder, his hair looking crazy, foaming at the mouth from running, his disturbingly pale skin rife with sweat, incoherent vocalizing, smashing into cars...Doxie looks certifiably insane.

Doxie steadies himself, turns around, and notices the police cars for the first time. Doxie is totally out of breath. Doxie tries to speak. He cannot. The officer in the K-9 unit gets out of his car. He lets Truman out of the car. Doxie again tries to speak. He's not sure why words aren't coming out. Doxie is in an altered state.

The K-9 officer restrains Truman by his leash and the other officers draw their service revolvers. Truman is barking his head off. The officer orders Doxie to lie down on the ground with his arms and legs spread out to the side. He tells him to do it right now. Doxie tries to explain to the officer that he needs to get back to the radio station before Jerry Nutter at Night throws away his chicken wings and steals his dog, but no words are coming out of his mouth. All Doxie can hear is the blood rushing in his head. The K-9 officer releases Truman.

Truman charges Doxie at full speed. Doxie's face fills with terror. The sound of the blood rushing in his head is very loud now. Doxie closes his eyes. Suddenly, Truman stops dead in his tracks. Truman sniffs Doxie and wags his tail. This freaks out the K-9 officer. This is not what Truman was trained to do. Nope. Not by a long shot.

After lingering only a moment, Truman runs by Doxie. Doxie, relieved and exhausted, passes out, falls flat on his face and shatters his nose. There is an amazing amount of blood, but at least he's not in any pain. That will come later, when he wakes up. Truman leaps into the trunk of the Mercedes. He pulls out the black suitcase and drags it out to the middle of the street. Truman rips the suitcase open and pulls out gallon size Ziploc bags filled to capacity with methamphetamine. Truman shreds the bags. The police officers are gob smacked. They call an ambulance for Doxie and the mobile crime lab for the biggest illegal drug investigation Midland City has ever seen. The police officers eagerly start to cordon off the area with copious amounts of official yellow crime scene tape.

Guido, Little Anthony and Big Anthony finish their ice cream. Guido, Little Anthony and Big Anthony stand up and walk towards the back door of the establishment. Guido gives the Mister Happy staff a hundred dollar bill and Little Anthony says, "Thank you very much" as they leave. They are picked up by Scully in the alley. Scully drives the milk truck. Scully was tailing them tonight, as per their usual protocol. Tonight is a prime example of why it's important for them to have usual protocol.

Guido, Little Anthony, Big Anthony and Scully will report what they've seen back to the rest of the mob. Calls will be made to Italy. Bonds will be tested. Backs will be stabbed. By the end of the week, there will be a new Boss running the Midland City Mob. Moreover, among the Midland City Mob, Valentino dresses will suddenly be out of style.

Yes, things just got interesting.

CHAPTER XX

Having taken his usual half an hour to meander three measly blocks, Alvin still sleeps peacefully as Jerry carries him down the hallway of the Sir William Old Folks' Home. Jerry walked right by the ruckus and hullabaloo outside. He is generally unnoticed and ignored wherever he goes.

Unlike outside, there is nothing interesting at the Sir William Old Folks' Home. Over the groans and the snores of the patients, Jerry hears the low voice of Mr. Black from one of the rooms about halfway down the hallway. Jerry needs to check in with Mr. Black every night so he doesn't go to jail. Jerry is nervous about bringing Alvin to work with him, but he has no choice.

The sadness in the hallway is palpable.

In Japan, old people are revered. They are treated with honor and dignity. Respect and admiration. But this is not Japan. This is Midland City. This is the Sir William Old Folks' Home. Here, people are treated with annoyance and disdain. Consternation and impudence. They are a burden on society. Medical science has caused the median age of death to keep increasing year after year. Old people don't seem to mind this too much, until they end up at the Sir William Old Folks' Home. Then they curse medical science. They scorn and openly and wantonly despise medical science. Sure, they are older than they thought that they would ever be, but their quality of life is shot to hell. They are forgotten. Dumped to finish wasting away in their own, lonely, private Hell. Out of sight and out of mind from the rest of society.

Jerry peers into the tiny room where the voice is emanating from and sees Mr. Black, the head Administrator for the home, standing at the foot of the bed. Mr. Black wears his customary black suit with black tie. Next to him are a doctor and a nurse that Jerry has seen, but never met. On the other side of the bed stands Moises, wearing his white coat, shirt and shoes. They all stand, looking at Ella, who lies motionless in the bed. Ella wears an old, cheap institutional nightgown and looks frail and weak. She appears to be gravely ill.

Ella is hooked up to a heart monitor. She has a copy of Shakespeare's complete works laying by her side. Her left hand strokes it so lightly that no one in the room can see her doing it. Jerry notices, though. Jerry is very observant. The heart monitor beeps.

Beep.

Beep.

Silence.

Beep.

Longer silence.

Beep.

The beeps get further and further apart.

"I'm checkin' in, Mister Black," says Jerry hesitantly, in a low yet loudish whisper. "Sorry I'm almost late."

"Yes, yes," responds Mr. Black hurriedly.

"Okay, then," says Jerry, surprised Mr. Black didn't notice Alvin.

Beep.

"We are busy here, Jerry," snips Mr. Black. "Go to Ward C and start on the bedpans."

Beep.

"But I emptied those yesterday," offers Jerry loudly, trying to remind Mr. Black of the three day bed-pan emptying schedule that Mr. Black's efficiency expert recommended. They save tens of dollars a week. Over time, that really adds up. For Mr. Black.

Beep.

"Go to Ward B. I don't care. Just get out," snaps Mr. Black.

"Yes sir," says Jerry. Jerry doesn't move.

Beep.

"How is she doing, Doc?" asks Moises to the doctor.

Beep.

"She is almost gone," says the doctor, gravely, glancing down at his wristwatch for effect.

Beep.

Moises looks at his wristwatch, but not only for effect. His motives are two-fold. Sure, he wants everyone in the room to see that he has a more expensive Rolex than the doctor does, but he also has an appointment. Ella can't die soon enough.

Suddenly, Alvin awakens. His ears perk up. His eyes radiate. His tail wags and every hair on his body tingles.

Alvin sees an aura through his cataracts. An energy. A light. It is his owner. Ella. It looks as though there is a golden halo around the top of her head. A crown. A lovely, golden crown. He has found her. His Queen. His Savior. His Owner. His Love. Ella. Finally.

Alvin barks.

Everyone in the room looks at Alvin.

Beep.

Beep.

Beep.

Alvin barks again.

Beep. Beep. Beep.

The beeps grow stronger and closer together. Alvin barks again.

"Alvin?" says Ella, coming out of her haze.

Everyone in the room is shocked.

"Hush, now, mother," says Moises, patting Ella's hand. "You are delirious. Just pass away in peace. Be with God. It's okay."

Alvin barks repeatedly and with great urgency.

"Shut that dog up!" shouts Moises to Jerry, frightening Jerry immensely. "Can't you see that a woman is dying in here?"

Jerry does his best to cover Alvin's mouth and get him not to bark. His tiny fingers combined with a complete lack of hand/eye coordination make his effort unsuccessful. Alvin barks and barks and barks and barks. And barks.

"Alvin!" shouts Ella. "It IS Alvin!"

Alvin barks even more. The beeps on the heart monitor are strong and regular.

"No it's not, Mother," says Moises. "You are imagining things."

Moises turns to the doctor and says, "The brain fever must have her in its grip. Her mind is gone."

"It that you, Moises?" asks Ella.

"Yes, Mother," whispers Moises with as much fake emotion as he can muster. "I am here with you. In your final moments on earth, and your time of need."

"I thought so," she responds.

Moises smiles smugly.

"Moises?" says Ella, with a whisper.

"Yes, dear Mother?" replies Moises in an equal whisper.

"My mind is fine!" shouts Ella with the authority and certainty of a Mother scorned. "And I may be blind, but I would know that bark anywhere! It's my dog, Alvin!"

Alvin barks and wags his tail furiously.

"Bring him here to me," orders Ella. Jerry gladly complies. Ella can barely contain Alvin as he licks her face.

"Alvin," says Ella. "It's my Alvin! I knew it!"

Alvin barks and wags his tail and licks Ella lovingly. He's back with his true love.

"No, Mother," says Moises. "It is a dog remarkably similar to Alvin. It's almost like...like...like it is Alvin's twin!"

Ella glares towards Moises with her blind eyes.

"You told me that Alvin died three days ago when you put me in this horrible place!" Ella shouts at him. "You told me that he got run over by a dump truck, you had him cremated, and that you were going to bury his ashes with me and we were going to be together FOREVER! You lied to me! You lied to me about Alvin and put me in this horrible place to die!"

And it is true. Moises knew that Ella had a dog, and that she would probably not be separated from it. But he had never seen the dog. He had not been inside his mother's house in almost 15 years. It was actually Moises' idea for her to get a dog. That way, she would have the dog to take care of and she would stay out of his business and she wouldn't mind that he never came over any more.

Moises knew that it was a small dog, as she had told him as much. He also knew that the dog's name was Alvin. That's because she would speak of him constantly when they would have their brief, sporadic telephone conversations.

When his Mother had her medical emergency three days ago and was rendered incapable of taking care of herself any longer, Moises was forced with making the decision of either having her come live with him at his home or putting her in "assisted living." He knew that there was only one real choice. He knew that she would never leave Alvin behind. So, Moises had the Midland City Ambulance Company come and pick up Ella and bring her to the Sir William home, promising to bring Alvin, himself, later that afternoon. Although discouraged, Ella was at least comforted by knowing that she didn't have to live with the son she hated and that Alvin would soon be joining her. She would live in a cardboard box on the street before she lived anywhere without her beloved Alvin. And Moises knew this. He knew there was no way that his mother was going to come to live with him, especially with a dog. He knew that if the media ever found out that his mother was living on the street, it would be a public relations disaster for his show. Moises knew that something had to be done. Something drastic.

Moises sent Jarious Jones, who happened to be dressed in a stunning Valentino metallic double wool and silk Empire coat and knit pencil skirt, to go pick up Alvin and take him out to the middle of a cornfield in the middle of nowhere in the middle of the night and leave him to die. Jarious Jones, a man of slightly more compassion than Moises, instead took the dog to the dog pound. Moises, true to form, never came that afternoon to see his Mother. He just called her on the phone and told her that Alvin was dead.

Ella made an amazingly rapid decline in health after she heard the news that Alvin was dead. It was as if she had lost the will to live. It was like that, because she had.

Mr. Black had tried to contact Moises several times about the condition of his Mother. He left multiple voice and text messages. But Moises was always too busy with other things, so he ignored them. All Moises knew was that she was still breathing. She was still alive. It was only when Mr. Black left him a message saying that the doctor thought that she would die any minute that Moises responded by immediately coming down to the Sir William Old Folks' Home to give the impression that he cared about her demise. Now, it looks like she will disappoint him.

"No, Mother," says Moises. "And this place isn't horrible. It's the best care that money can buy!"

"I may be blind," seethes Ella, "but my other senses are intact, you idiot. This place smells like vomit and urine and the staff is drunk and mean and there are people in PAIN and nobody CARES!"

Mr. Black turns to Moises and whispers, "We are working on the smell..."

"And with all the money you have, Moises," continues Ella, "this is the best that you could do for me? For your own mother? You are a rotten son!"

"Hush now, mother," says Moises with embarrassment. "You are dying, remember?"

"She seems to be making a miraculous recovery," says the doctor.

The nurse nods in agreement.

"Look," says Moises, noticing the time and realizing that his Mother is not going to die, "I have a meeting really soon. Perhaps I should just get going..."

"You would have me die here, ALONE-" shouts Ella.

"But I'm here, Mother," says Moises. "See? You are not alone."

Moises looks at his wristwatch again and taps his foot impatiently.

"You are only here because you think I am going to die!" retorts Ella. "Where have you been for the past three days?!"

"I'm a busy man, Mother," says Moises, explaining and justifying his absence more to the people in the room than to Ella.

"Don't give me that!" shouts Ella.

"I know that you are busy, Moises," says Mr. Black.

"Give me a BREAK! His name isn't 'Moises.' It's Bart! Bart Smith! You were born Bart Smith! Then something happened! You got greedy! You loved money more than anything! More than your own mother! You became an awful, awful man!" shouts Ella.

Alvin wags his tail.

"And you lied to me about Alvin!" she continues. "After everything I've done for you! I GAVE YOU LIFE, YOU IDIOT!!! I raised you! By myself! After your father left! Is that why all of this has happened? Because you didn't have a good, strong father figure in your life? Well, I did the best that I could! I sacrificed for you! I dedicated my entire life to you! And this is how you repay me?! Taking my dog away and dumping me in here!?!?! This is NOT the son that I raised!"

"I am a man of GOD, Mother," says Moises, patiently.

"What God? The God of money and shame?" shouts Ella.

"Mother," whispers Moises, "can we talk about this in private for a minute?"

"I want you out of my life forever!" shouts Ella.

Sargent Bradley and Detective Abromowitz appear at the doorway. They have come inside as part of their investigation outside. They heard all of the commotion coming from the room and decided to investigate.

"Good evening," says Mr. Black, nodding to the badges and authority. "May I help you?"

"Is everything okay in here?" asks Sargent Bradley. "We heard yelling from down the hall."

"It's all under control. There's nothing to worry about in here," says Mr. Black, not really sure if it IS all under control or not, but that is Mr. Black's standard response to everything.

"Okay. Good," says Detective Abromowitz. "You know, I was wondering, do you know who that Mercedes parked out front belongs to?"

"Does the license plate say "FAITH'A"?" asks Moises.

"Why, yes," says Sargent Bradley with great interest. "Yes it does."

"That's my car, officer," says Moises with the definite sin of pride and then a sudden tinge of concern.

"Did you know that the trunk is open?" asks Detective Abromowitz flatly.

Moises' eyes get wide with panic. Everyone looks at him.

"That black suitcase is NOT mine," blurts Moises awkwardly. "I have nothing to do with that meth! Someone must have planted it there!"

"Who said anything about a black suitcase?" asks Detective Abromowitz.

"And who said anything about methamphetamine?" asks Sargent Bradley.

"Are you psychic?" asks Detective Abromowitz with a certain degree of joy.

"I...uh..." stammers Moises.

"And what's your name, sir?" asks Detective Abromowitz with an even greater degree of joy. This is why he became a detective in the first place.

To bust people who think they are smarter than he is, and who think they can get away with anything.

"Sir?" Detective Abromowitz asks again. "Your name?"

"I would have no idea," says Moises, his brain running wild with panic.

"But that IS your Mercedes out front," clarifies Sargent Bradley.

"Uhhhh..." stammers Moises. He is at a total loss for words and, since that never happens to him, he is also frightened.

"Get him OUT of here!" shouts Ella.

Alvin barks and wags his tail.

"Why don't we go outside and have a little talk, sir," says Detective Abromowitz to Moises, taking him by the arm and leading him out into the hallway.

"You see, officers," explains Moises, "I am a man of God."

"Uh huh," says Sargent Bradley.

"Are you familiar with God?" asks Moises.

"Why, yes," says Sargent Bradley. "As a matter of fact, I meet people every day who claim to be God. Do you claim to be God?"

"No," says Moises with defeat and resignation.

"Well," says Sargent Bradley, laughing. "That's a relief. And please keep your hands where I can see them."

"Of course," says Moises, sheepishly, trying desperately to remember the phone number of his lawyer as he is lead down the hallway and outside to the squad car.

Ella remains in the room with Jerry, Alvin, Mr. Black, the doctor and the nurse. Alvin, exhausted from his adventure, has fallen asleep in Ella's arms.

"How are you feeling, Ella?" asks the doctor.

"Now that I have my Alvin back," she says, "I feel like a new woman. Thank you."

"All right then," says the doctor. "We will be going. Nurse?"

The doctor nods to the nurse and they leave the room.

"Look," says Jerry to nobody in particular. "Alvin is sleeping."

"He's such a good boy," says Ella. "He's never even been the slightest bit of trouble. I am so happy that he is back, my heart feels like it is going to burst!"

"Now you just get some sleep yourself, Ella," says Mr. Black. "And have a good night, okay Ella?"

"Yes," says Ella. "I will."

Mr. Black and Jerry walk into the hallway. They turn around and watch Ella and Alvin.

Ella closes her eyes and immediately falls asleep, a huge smile on her face. She is perfectly content.

"It's a shame that you don't allow pets here, Mr. Black," says Jerry. "Alvin sure seems to make her happy."

"We allow pets here, Jerry," corrects Mr. Black.

"Well," questions Jerry, "how come nobody has one?"

"It costs an extra 20 dollars a week," explains Mr. Black. "When children place their parents here, they don't want to pay for that."

Jerry looks at Mr. Black. Jerry pulls out his wallet and offers Mr. Black a 20-dollar bill. Mr. Black smiles, refuses the money, and walks away.

Jerry looks back in to the room. Alvin opens his left eye and looks at Jerry. Jerry cocks an eyebrow. Jerry smiles. Alvin smiles in his heart and falls asleep. Jerry turns and walks down the hall, off to empty bedpans for the next several hours before he has to go back to work.

Ella and Alvin sleep in bliss.

All is again right in the world.

And they live happily ever after.